Ava Kadishson Schieber

present
past

NORTHWESTERN UNIVERSITY PRESS

EVANSTON, ILLINOIS

Northwestern University Press
www.nupress.northwestern.edu

Text and drawings copyright © 2016 by Ava Kadishson Schieber. Foreword
copyright © 2016 by Danny M. Cohen. Published 2016 by Northwestern
University Press. All rights reserved.

Printed in the United States of America

10 9 8 7 6 5 4 3 2 1

Library of Congress Cataloging-in-Publication Data

Names: Schieber, Ava Kadishson, author. | Cohen, Danny M., writer of foreword.
Title: Present past / Ava Kadishson Schieber ; with a foreword by Danny M.
  Cohen.
Description: Evanston, Illinois : Northwestern University Press, 2016.
Identifiers: LCCN 2016007595| ISBN 9780810133792 (pbk. : alk. paper) |
  ISBN 9780810134669 (cloth : alk. paper)
Subjects: LCSH: Schieber, Ava Kadishson. | Poets, American—20th century—
Biography. | Holocaust, Jewish (1939–1945)—Yugoslavia. | Jewish women—
United States—Biography. | Holocaust, Jewish (1939–1945)—Poetry. | Artists—
United States—Biography. | Jews—Yugoslavia—Poetry.
Classification: LCC PS3619.C357 Z46 2016 | DDC 811/.6—dc23
LC record available at http://lccn.loc.gov/2016007595

present
past

Contents

Foreword

The high school students rush into the auditorium, some excited, some apprehensive to hear artist and writer Ava Kadishson Schieber.

Most have never before heard a Holocaust survivor speak. Many of these teenagers, African American and Latino public school students on Chicago's South Side, have never met a Jew, until today. The room is full and buzzing with adolescent chatter while a few students sit quietly, staring at the white-haired eighty-something-year-old woman at the front of the vast room.

As Ava takes a step forward, the teachers make sharp shushing sounds and the room falls quiet. Some students seem nervous, perhaps because in their classrooms they have already watched video clips of Holocaust survivor testimonies. They are expecting to hear the old woman's story, accompanied by her tears.

"So, what do you want to know?" are Ava's first words.

The students are frozen in silence. They seem surprised. There is no introduction, no rehearsed narrative. Ava does not stand on the stage, but in front of it. She smiles and begins to walk between the rows of seats.

"You can ask me anything."

One student raises his hand. The conversation is about to begin, as Ava had planned, with each student in the director's chair.

"How old are you?" he asks.

The room holds its breath, nervous that he has asked an inappropriate question.

"I am fifteen," is Ava's immediate reply.

The students seem both confused and amused. Soft laughter fills the space and the ice is broken.

The young people have questions about Ava's childhood in Novi Sad, Yugoslavia, and about her four years in hiding from the Nazis on a farm close to Belgrade.

"How did you deal with your grief after your sister's death?"

"After the Nazis killed your father in Auschwitz, did you want revenge?"

They offer smart interpretations of Ava's drawings and poetry in her first book, *Soundless Roar*, in which she recalls her wartime experiences as a teen. Her childhood was stolen from her, she explains to the fascinated students, and they are reminded of Ava's insistence that she is fifteen years old.

Ava's answers are unexpected. She weaves specific retellings of moments on the farm where "I played a deaf mute" between abstracted reflections on the significance of her survival. She offers advice to the students on dealing with trauma and loss and then reminds them of the persistence of antisemitism. Eloquent yet improvised, Ava answers a student's question about the loss of childhood with a reply about her own parenthood. When a student asks about bereavement in the context of genocide, Ava responds with a short reflection on becoming a widow many decades after the Second World War.

After forty minutes, the high schoolers and their teachers have come to see that Ava's memories are not linear. A memory from her early childhood is embedded within a memory of living in Communist Europe, which is in turn connected to a memory from her life as an artist and theater set designer in 1950s Israel, where many survivors of the Holocaust experienced both compassion and marginalization. And these entwined tales lead Ava back to talk about her father's decision to split up their Jewish family and go into hiding to avoid Nazi deportation.

Just as the lines in Ava's drawings connect the figures and faces that filled and disappeared from her life, her writings place stories within stories that loop and turn and fold back on themselves. Some students ask if Ava's writing is fiction. The answer is that the content of each story is truthful, but its structure has been imagined by Ava and its accompanying art and poetry have been carefully arranged. For she is an expert in theatrical design, adept at delivering restrained frames, convincing sceneries, and painted backdrops to support honest storytelling.

While Ava's debut *Soundless Roar* focuses on her time during the war, *Present Past* takes its readers many years beyond the Nazi era, yet sometimes slips back to it, to construct a narrative that addresses the significance of its unending aftermath. This perspective is rare within the genre of Holocaust testimony, memoir, and autobiography. Thousands of survivors of Nazism have written and recorded their experiences leading up to, during, and in the immediate wake of the Holocaust, but few focus their narratives on the challenges and triumphs of survivorship and the reconstruction of life.

In the many stories, poems, and artworks of *Present Past*, we follow Ava out of hiding, through the period of Allied liberation, and into Soviet-occupied south central Europe where, reunited with her mother, Ava makes plans to immigrate to the newly founded State of Israel and, decades later, the United States. All the while, we trace Ava's training in Belgrade and Prague, her accomplishments as a set designer in the theaters of Tel Aviv, and as an artist in the galleries of New York.

But this is not a rags-to-riches tale. Throughout her stories and poems, again and again, Ava in the postwar era befriends and gives the stage to individuals who have their own hidden truths and their own wounds to heal. *Present Past* evokes the works of other Holocaust writers, including Charlotte Delbo who, in *Auschwitz and After*, reconstructs voices of murdered comrades and those who survived and suffered. Through postwar encounters with other veterans, Ava the survivor becomes witness and through her writing and art she is both liberator and reporter as she directs the spotlight on others who suffered wartime atrocities, ongoing oppression, and secret abuse. As Ava carries memories of her adolescence, she absorbs the stories of fellow wayfarers and integrates their experiences within her own narrative.

When recalling memories of a destroyed Europe, the immediacy of Ava's writing signals the trepidation of the refugee. Some of Ava's words, and sometimes the order of words, are peculiar, unexpected, jarring. Ava writes in English, although she did not learn English until later in life. Yet, we come to see that, just as her responses to students' questions are intentionally elusive, Ava is in command of her craft. The strangeness of her chosen words are at once deliberate and an echo of her traumatic experiences. Woven into the urgency of Ava's testimony, in words but also through her abstract line drawings, charcoal impressions, and paintings, is a discourse on how memory works.

Yet, Ava makes clear, remembering is not an easy task. In her untitled poem placed before the story "Soap Bubbles," Ava suggests that the memory of an emotion, like a soap bubble, "will rupture at the touch." As she attempts to find the words to express her wordless memories of hurt and of love, the progression of Ava's stories, poems, and visual art mirrors her confrontations with trauma and an eventual acceptance of her pain and shattering losses.

After conducting their unplanned interview with Ava, the high school students exit the auditorium with an impression that a survivor's present is saturated by the past. As Ava writes in her story "The Olive Tree," "I have seen what is now in the archives for historians. Those images flooded my entire brain. I never can remove those deposited atrocities from my memory." While *Soundless Roar* provides its young and adult readers with an essential account of a teenager's experiences in hiding from Hitler's murderers, Ava Kadishson Schieber's *Present Past* presents a lifetime of scenes played out before a constant backdrop and unchanging scenery that she did not design.

—Danny M. Cohen

Acknowledgments

Love and gratitude. These are the dominant sentiments crowding my mind after all is said, and suddenly words become woefully inadequate. Thanksgiving fed the source of energy throughout the many decades in whatever I did and created. I was given love and taught gratitude by those who improved me. They eagerly handed me the most essential tools of how to build my life; deal with central and random ordeals; help me meet challenges.

I am grateful for the uplifting memories of the loving partners who joined my life's journey, thankful for their emotional honesty and the intellectual abundance they generously shared, without trying to change me—presenting the ultimate proof in love.

I am profoundly thankful to my children and grandchildren in their mature understanding and acceptance of my intricate need for personal isolation, which has never lessened the bonds of love, respect, and shared joy in our individual creativity.

Throughout my journey I feel awarded with intimate friends. The gracious facilitation of Professor Phyllis Lassner goaded me through the writing of my first and second books. As a generous educator she suggested her doctoral student Danny M. Cohen to edit *Present Past*. Besides language proficiency, my writing gained more lucidity as I worked with someone of my grandchildren's generation. I am the witness of my own experiences and the owner of my memory fragments. But Danny's reactions to my writing allowed me to be more unclouded. It was indeed an invigorating task that added meaning to my summing up at my present onset of sunset.

—*Ava Kadishson Schieber*

present
past

distance from the onset of my personal experiences enormously lengthened

the road ahead is a notably shrinking prospective reality

carried through time streams seeds of yesteryear

germinate and sprout

within the drying riverbed

of memory

Flightless Birds

"It had been an unfortunate accident" was the summing up of the event.

For all of us it was a painful reality. Mickey was dead. Everyone who investigated what had happened concluded that unfortunate omissions led to the fatal accident. Mickey wore glasses; people said his poor vision probably caused the tragedy. The glasses were found beside the elevator shaft on the top floor of the building under construction. Perhaps he removed them or they fell off. All the shafts on the lower floors, which usually were securely covered, were left uncovered that evening. What was exposed was a drop of several floors all the way to the basement. The investigation concluded that the unsecured elevator passage was the serious security breach that caused Mickey's death. We were left with the question: had someone intentionally removed all the safety covers? If someone asked, no one answered.

The night watchman who arrived late for work that evening said he didn't see anyone going in or coming out of the construction site, nor did he hear anything. Mickey might have been crushed on the basement floor before the tardy watchman's arrival. My recurring thought was that I hoped he died instantly, because it frightened me to imagine my Mickey slowly dying in the darkness, alone and in pain.

Only part-time electricity was installed in the building. It was in the morning when the construction workers arrived for work that Mickey's shattered body was discovered on the bottom floor of the basement. It was assumed that Mickey the young architect must have arrived at dusk after the construction crew had finished work on the concrete for the top floor. In his meticulous way Mickey would always conduct daily inspections of how the work progressed. It was also Mickey's habit to take samples to inspect the mixed concrete to be poured between floors.

I remember some of the family lawyers complaining about an ongoing negligence which had caused the fatality. Light bulbs were missing in the hallways leading to the elevators where there should have been emergency illumination at night. There were no explanations for the combined negligence. The official conclusion to the tragic accident was simply that there were multiple unfortunate omissions that had caused Mickey's death.

In the mid 1930s in the urban community of Novi Sad most houses had two or three floors. This new building, in 1932, was to be the first multiple-floor high-rise for our town. Elevators were the new urban luxury for Novi Sad. They were a sign of keeping pace with modern innovations. Mickey Handler, our second cousin, had started his career after concluding his exams with honors in central Europe, perhaps Vienna. Mickey was working on the large new urban project as a rising star. All of us in the family were very proud that he was awarded the role of planning such a prestigious high-rise.

I loved Mickey's gentle manner, his unassuming air. Bright and funny, he was never conceited about his talent or knowledge. Mickey always took time to answer me patiently. As a small girl, I could not yet explain it, but to me Mickey represented what a man was supposed to be. A father was once a role model of masculinity, for how a girl viewed the opposite sex. I admired my father's sophisticated explanations, his way of telling jokes, his entertaining ditties which were on the edge of bon ton. But Mickey was different. He represented and embodied serenity. In later years I recognized how he became the model of how I judged men. I imagined if Mickey were alive, how he would behave in a given situation. His image guided me to either accept or reject a relationship.

After his death my older sister Susan and I talked about the deep pain of our loss. People who had died in our family were old, and even if we liked some of the deceased, their deaths were a part of nature. Mickey was young, full of joy, and we loved him. His death was cruel and felt vicious.

At first people talked a lot about the accident. Some people from our large extended family said Mickey was too conscientious and should not have taken such meticulous care in supervising details at work. Those comments of my elders opposed what we children had always been taught. We were constantly urged to do the very best we could. Mickey did just that and was killed in the process while checking the progress of the day's work. When gossip began to blame Mickey for being overly conscientious about the high quality in his project, the entire criticism began to sound off-key.

Then the rumors started to circulate about coworkers' resentments. Each time the concrete was being poured, Mickey would take samples of it. Were there improprieties regarding the building materials?

Of course the source for most of our information was George, who was Mickey's cousin and Susan's and my second cousin. George became the main bearer of rumors, gossip, and all notable news items he usually acquired while eavesdropping. The tragic accident was a local sensation and besides his personal relationship with Mickey, George had his own vivid imagination. George Szekely probably was around Mickey's age, but no one ever compared them. George had a law degree but did not work in his father's law office. The Szekely family lived almost across the street from our house; therefore we were in close contact. Susan, my older sister, formed a team with George in finding out more information about the tragedy that involved all of us. I tried to keep pace with them and was happy they did not exclude me.

It might have been a month after the accident when there were veiled insinuations about some contractor's misuse of cement in the concrete. George was sure that Mickey's meticulous samples for analysis prompted someone to stop him from finding proof of corruption. Strangely, when the story started buzzing around the entire affair, talks about the accident rapidly faded.

There were no more articles in the papers. The sensation of the young architect's death dissipated. His first project was his last. Soon the entire event fell into a void. The community's interest waned, and other news dominated the front pages. Our family lawyers also ended their activities; Susan and George talked about that. What mostly escaped me at that time were allegations I could not understand. There were those many question marks that showed in the worried facial expressions of grown-ups, leaving me tantalized. Therefore the tragedy about Mickey's death was hanging in midair. I started to dream about Mickey floating in the Danube and then I would see him crushed on a stone floor, the crowd around the open grave, earth covering his coffin. That dream hounded me, and the reluctance of grown-ups to answer clearly what I wanted to know began a scary uncertainty in my mind about Mickey's death. Even Susan and George either withheld information or probably did not know and were therefore silent. I was introduced to sensing evil and violent death and left to find my own interpretation to solve my fears.

During that school year Susan contracted scarlet fever and I had to leave my home to prevent getting ill. I could not attend school or have contact with any children so as not to transfer the infection. My quarantine was for a couple of weeks at the Szekelys', George's home in the Zeleznitcka Ulica. It soon became clear to me that George was already busy with other activities and without Susan he probably considered me too young to be a partner in pursuing any further inquiries about Mickey's death. Although in a very friendly house but not in the familiar room I shared with Susan whom I missed, I felt alone. I found solace in George's dogs and his birds. George had an entire porch closed into an enormous birdcage for his numerous parakeets so they were almost free. That porch overlooked a large garden stretching in the back of their house. I loved the huge trees and overgrown garden, the three dogs running around with me. The nature lover in George was what I liked and most felt comfortable with.

In our conservative extended family George was labeled immature and extravagant. George expressed himself in the swinging art deco style, with its artificial euphoric gaiety. He emulated the lifestyle of people who did not work for a living, but only enjoyed their hobbies. There was a youthful prankster in George. Maybe that was why Susan and I loved him.

If I recall those enclosing conservative attitudes as part of the eventful atmosphere of my childhood, I see a heap of multicolored elements as if looking into a kaleidoscope of a distant reality. The fragments become necessary parts to reconstruct my memory mosaic. I admit there are missing elements in my imaging; even in my paintings I leave blank spaces on the canvas to represent the past for which I have no details or distinct color.

Mickey and George's grandfather Shimon was my great-uncle. I viewed Shimon and his wife Risa as an unlikely couple, yet they procreated three daughters. Shimon was Grandmother's oldest brother and he was often derogated in Hungarian as *a parast*, which meant "the peasant." All the closer family members were city dwellers. Though some were more educated than others, they all tried to be socially impressive. Risa preferred the city as the farm life disagreed with her, she constantly claimed. Shimon and I shared a love of horses and animals in general. Because his wife deeply disliked animals, I thought this was true of everything around her. Two of Shimon and Risa's daughters had their mother's all-suffering facial expression. Ella, the oldest, Mickey's mother, obviously happy and proud of her son, was the only one with a beautiful smile. Even as a child I noticed how his untimely death changed her from a beauty to a wilting, fading woman. She and her husband did not live in Novi Sad before the tragedy. After the inquiries into Mickey's death ended, they stopped visiting the family who lived there. Ella's husband might have been related or just had the same family name. I could never really figure out the large clan of the

Handlers and the Hershels. There were those I liked and others I did not care about.

Ella's younger sister Jenny, George's mother, was married to Jeno Szekely, a man Susan and I liked very much. He was a lawyer who frequently took on clients with no means to pay his fees. He was known for his generosity, which his wife did not share. Some family members were confusing and others boring.

The youngest of Shimon and Risa's daughters, Julia, had two daughters who were younger than I. The Shoenbergers, I was told, married late as Julia waited for the man she loved to finish his medical studies. I wondered why any woman would wait for that man. To me as a child Dr. Schoenberger seemed utterly disagreeable, cold, and pompous. I tried not to complain about any physical discomfort, as he was our family physician. I always disliked him and that did not improve later on, but intensified.

During that early period I absorbed the episodes around me. I eagerly listened, mostly without understanding. When Mickey was with Susan and me, he would talk about the Bauhaus influence on architecture and the visual arts, even the contemporary music of Europe. When Mickey was gone and I could not ask him anymore for explanations, I started reading books about art history in search for answers. Reading about art kept Mickey in my thoughts.

Susan and I had a close bond. Together we planned and chose contemporary furniture for our shared room. Maybe the five-year age difference eliminated any competition between us. My parents although attentive and patient were somewhat in the background.

After experiencing war I could reconstruct and understand my parents' apparently detached behavior in that loaded tense atmosphere of the 1930s. I was not aware of their trepidations about the brewing toxicity of demagogy and antisemitism which like an enormous tidal wave was flooding our existence. A child just breathes in all the media pollutants and paddles through the infested waters of politically deceptive machinations of the churning fanatical nationalism. I may have even developed antibodies and a lifelong immunity against the epidemics of hate.

Perhaps my good luck was my older sister Susan who talked to me about her more urgent fears of what was already happening in Germany. Her seniority helped her understand my fears when I told her about my dreams connected with Mickey's death. What did he feel during his fall? How did death feel?

Never before was I afraid to fall from a horse or a high place. Susan knew that I used to climb out of our attic window leading to the roof, close to the bench for the chimney sweeper. I would sit on that bench and watch birds flying by. I used to enjoy that but stopped. Obsessing about Mickey's accident, I started to connect falling from heights and the basements of the city buildings with death. It was a relief to tell Susan those fears. I was very troubled that no one talked about Mickey anymore. Mickey was forgotten.

I view vignettes from distant childhood like raw precious stones. As hourglass sand seeps and polishes their surfaces, and as time and personal maturity modify how we view those events, the sand creates multiple angles that illuminate the details. Those memories transform into heirlooms.

Early on I knew that Mother came from a Roman Catholic family and she chose to convert to Judaism. From time to time Mother told Susan and me details from her childhood. We knew that her own mother had died when she was seven. Mother was not as eloquent as Grandmother could be, but there was a sincere simplicity I understood from her answers to my inquisitiveness. Mother had left the church in utter disillusionment. She lost the trust she depended upon after losing her mother. The priest she regularly confessed to since childhood tried to molest her. Mother walked away from this deception and dishonesty. For us children it was part of Mother's decisiveness. That might have encouraged me to be firm and fast in my lifelong decisions.

What brought change and excitement to my silent mourning of Mickey's death was that Mother planned to take Susan and me to Vienna where I was going to meet her sisters Kate and Steffi. This would be Susan's second time in the big city. All other recollections of Vienna the city, even the Prater with its giant Ferris wheel, somewhat paled in comparison to Gaveinstahl, the village where Aunt Kate, the oldest of the sisters, lived. Aunt Steffi, on vacation from her work at the children's hospital, accompanied us and stayed for a couple of days. Kate, Mother, and Steffi had seemed very happy in their reunion. Kate and her husband Hans Leitner, the principal of the village school, lived in a nice house with a lovely vegetable garden. Because their children were younger than I was, I felt somewhat worldlier. Susan, a teenager, was mostly reading while I tried to find a way to communicate with my cousins. I was fluent in German but their behavior was much more restricted or timid; maybe they were more polite than I was.

This was the pre-Nazi era, but there were already signs that put my youthful sense of security in disarray, exposing my defiance. I liked Uncle Hans because he loved animals. He was breeding the most beautiful roosters I had ever seen. As an educator he recognized my interest in his beautiful, colorful birds. Whenever Uncle Hans appeared, they all responded to his voice by crowing at the same time. For me this was more than amusement. When I told Uncle Hans about my watching the storks' nests on the roofs in our neighborhood as I sat on the bench of our chimney sweeper, and cousin George's parakeets back in Novi Sad, Uncle Hans let me accompany him when he fed his birds in the mornings. One morning the whole feeding ceremony turned into a sinister experience. One of the roosters was lying outside its coop with his throat cut. That sight locked Gaveinstahl vividly into my memory. Mother, Susan, and I were there when someone started killing Uncle Hans's marvelous roosters, one by one.

I remember how I felt each morning as Uncle Hans would weep about another slain bird. I shared his pain, seeing a man cry, and felt my own fear of a powerful evil that continued even after the last rooster was killed.

Sadly I do not recollect what Uncle Hans said, but I remember how he looked in those days. The tall burly man with red cheeks would suddenly get pale, as if all color was escaping from his face, and that was frightening. What I understood at that time was that Hans opposed the rise of a new political party in the village, the National Socialists. Hans, a school principal who belonged to the Catholic Democrats, was a powerful opponent. Aunt Kate talked about it in front of us children and it induced a foreboding atmosphere.

In that troubled unease, Mother, Susan, and I left Austria. Not long after we were back in Novi Sad, Mother received a letter with a black rimmed envelope from Aunt Kate telling us that Uncle Hans had died from a heart attack.

I remember Uncle Hans burying the roosters in his garden in Gaveinstahl. For me it was wicked to kill birds that belonged to someone who loved them. I felt that there was danger, evil, and growing cruelty surrounding us. I did not yet understand the symbolic meaning behind the killing of roosters.

BETWEEN THE AGE of ten and eleven, in the late 1930s, I started the first year of high school. That was when Steffi, Mother's younger sister, became engaged to be married in Vienna. Her fiancé was Jewish, and of course Susan and I were excited about our journey to attend the wedding and we joked that the sisters, our mother and Steffi, both had chosen their husbands to have the same name—Leo. Susan and I were preoccupied with choosing our dresses for the wedding in Vienna. Then the unforeseen occurred.

Leo, Steffi's fiancé, was killed, falling from the high-rise window of his apartment in Vienna. The police declared the young Jewish jeweler's death an accident. Steffi arrived heartbroken in Novi Sad to be with us, her family, to help her emotionally. She did not spare herself or us in revealing what she knew. When she arrived at Leo's apartment it was ransacked and in utter disorder. The floor was littered with books and contents of drawers, Leo's desk was broken, the bed comforter and pillows cut, as well as Leo's clothing and all upholstery slashed. Whoever pushed Leo to his death had searched for what Steffi said Leo never had. Leo did not own any precious items. He worked in a jewelry shop and created objects in cloisonné. He was an artist. There were no valuables in Leo's and her future apartment, Steffi said. The Viennese authorities disregarded that vicious event. There were no further inquiries about the young Jewish man's death and his ransacked home.

The policeman who was on the premises when Steffi arrived told the distraught bride-to-be that she should not get involved with Jews but find an Aryan suitor.

We were sad and troubled by what Steffi was telling us. The intensifying attacks on Jews, with authorities openly condoning murder, predicted a menacing future. At the same time world leaders were assuring peace.

Aunt Steffi stayed with us for several weeks to recover from her loss. A somber future was expanding. Steffi's Leo, the artist, had been creating precious objects. Steffi, a registered nurse specializing in premature infant care, was maintaining precious but endangered life. Steffi never married.

ON APRIL 6, 1941, in the open season of war, Nazi Germany's bombers started to destroy Belgrade. The undefended city with more than half a million inhabitants had its entire water and electricity system shattered in the first day's relentless bombardments. Day and night, waves of bombs were exploding in Belgrade, and they remained vivid in my mind through the years, the many decades, my lifetime. I recorded it in paintings, with words, videotapes, lectures. My past retains an immediate present in my recollections.

MY FIRST PERSONAL experience of war was that nonstop onslaught, explosions, incineration, absolute chaos, lawlessness. I refused to take shelter in the basement of our high-rise building in Belgrade. I had to be outside the cellar close to the exit to the street. Father, a veteran of the First World War, tried to convince me that the air pressure of explosions was lethal and so was flying debris. I knew he was right, but when I told him that my worst fear was to be buried alive in a basement, he stood beside me, finding shelter just behind a wall, able to see the sky and breathe open air. For me a cellar did not represent a shelter but a trap. It was like Mickey's tomb. I realized my fear of death was less threatening in the open where I could face the danger.

My fear of death felt less suffocating if instantaneous, I told Father. He did not insist that I follow his rationale. I was making my decisions about my life as a fully grown person from that moment on. Father reassured me that it was right to listen to my emotions and let them take the lead in whatever situation I was going to face in the future. I was on my own to decide and act.

Of course, at fifteen I did not understand why Father gave in to my need. But I forever cherish his deep understanding of my fear that had started in my childhood, leaving me with neither illusions nor conclusions.

between daydreams and nightmares

is the fine line I decided to walk

the tightrope

a long rod in my hands loss and hope on opposite ends

keeping balance

with no safety net

a fall is all it takes

yet

there is no other chance

to advance

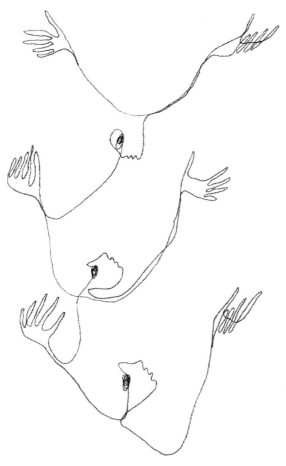

Messenger

we were deprived of benefitting from

a milder season's amenities

we laced few days of youthful glow

and I still feel that bold embrace

as cold flurries race

beyond my windowsill

A letter delivered by messenger was an extraordinary wartime event. In 1944, with a life of its own, the war was still fully engrossed in its drive to kill. After the withdrawal of Nazi combat units, I was living in an area of relative calm in Belgrade, but even at a distance we were well informed about the fierce ongoing fighting. Battles continued to rage on the fronts and sometimes the back alleys as well. Partisans and Russian military convoys of soldiers and tanks were moving north out of Belgrade. Because the hospitals were overcrowded with wounded soldiers, makeshift infirmaries were established in schools and public buildings.

Like my mother, there were some middle-aged women who had either converted to Judaism or had intermarried with Jews, and who had not been denounced. There was the neighbor who lived across the street from Mother, Mrs. Mileva, who was a Sephardic Jew married to a Greek Orthodox Christian.

During the war, Mother and Mileva kept silent about their identities when they often met standing in the long lines for the meager rations. When the German Army left the city, the women revealed what they had suspected yet did not dare to talk about. Emerging out of her hiding, Mileva connected to the prewar active Jewish community center in Belgrade. She instigated the group of women volunteers, including my mother, to work at the food distribution and kitchen of the center. There was no one my age at that time in the group of women, which also served in the improvised hospital headed by Dr. Alcalay. I tried to help because war had been such an intense part of my life.

Like so many, I veered between feeling immediate distrust and caution when a stranger suddenly stood at the door. This time it was a Russian soldier. With the reign of death still dominating the foreground, any feeling of security disappeared. For years, staying afloat had demanded swift decisiveness.

I was facing a Russian soldier, a presence that could not have been anticipated. What we did know was that the Russian Army was suspect, because its often drunk soldiers were constantly inciting fights. We heard circulating stories of assaults on civilians and rapes, perpetrated by the soldiers, of women of any age. Those rumors were like fire, expanding through the winds of fears. The Russians were therefore avoided by the local population. But so were all strangers avoided, especially armed soldiers. As if this weren't enough, the appearance of this soldier at my door was also startling because of the Soviets' position at this time of the war. As the Communists solidified their position in the Balkans, the Red Army was in transit, and the fighters usually kept their distance from civilians.

The young man standing in my doorway was dressed in a torn combat uniform caked with mud. His jacket was open; I did not notice any weapon, which was my first concern. In one hand the soldier carried his crumpled hat, in the other an envelope smeared with mud. The face of a boy was on top of his tattered shirt. His cheeks had dark smudges and scratches exposed by being too young to shave. My eyes were immediately drawn to my name, written in large handwriting on the center of the mud-smeared envelope. All this made me more curious about who had written to me. Who had sent him? How did he know where I lived? What I recognized instantly was that the writer was not my missing sister or father. Because I knew their handwriting so well, and this writing was so unlike theirs, my surging hope dissipated immediately. I put the letter into my pocket, as I wanted to read it before telling my mother about its existence. I knew Mother was not going to come to see who was at the door. She would sit in her chair, reading books. She had developed an attitude somewhat removed from life and surrounding events. I didn't know if the four years of war had caused her withdrawal or if I had different expectations when we reunited after our long separation. I felt I had to shield her from additional hurt, represented by the postwar reality.

Hidden for years on a small farm with only occasional forays into the city, I had learned that a written document was either lifesaving or endangering. I was supposed to be a peasant girl with no education at all, a story that my rescuers made known to the neighbors. Outside the farm I was a deaf mute girl, hired to work at the beginning of the war. A handicapped person was usually avoided by all, even the curious peasants. People's superstitions became an additional cloak covering my existence.

Ever since the occupation began in 1941, among all the regions of the Balkans, Serbia had been singled out by the Germans for special punishment. Yugoslavia had been created a monarchy after the Armistice in 1918.

The treaties that had unified different ethnic groups fell apart in the spring of 1941. After one generation, this disintegration allowed the German Army to march through Slovenia and Croatia with little resistance. In some areas they were even greeted with flowers. There was one armed opposition. The units of Draza Michaelovic, a Serbian general, never stopped fighting the occupiers. Serbia and its population had declared its clandestine war. The 1942 fighting in Serbia escalated when the partisans of the Soviet-backed Joseph Broz Tito suddenly appeared. The Germans' harsh punishments were meted out to the Serb population and lasted throughout the entire occupation.

At the very beginning of the Nazi invasion, all the registered Jews of Serbia were killed. The peasants who gave me shelter when I was on the run were Macedonian political exiles of previous unrests who had escaped to Serbia. They were fiercely independent and hated the merciless occupier. I was fortunate to have met people who were ready to risk their lives to defy a formidable enemy. However, the four years of hiding on their farm turned me into an old woman of nineteen.

The soldier at the door looked really young, but it didn't occur to me that he might have been my age. As I scrutinized him for a moment he said: "The letter is from Stephan." I invited him in. My mother and I inhabited a section in an apartment we shared with two other families, but we enjoyed the benefit of a separate entrance. Our neighbors, so close yet strangers, were two families of Czarist Russian refugees who had escaped the Bolshevik Revolution many decades before. Some of their aged family members had carried their memories with them. Transmitting the fears embedded in their memories, they inspired anxieties in the younger generation who lived in dread of the Red Army.

I was glad my neighbors did not see the soldier I invited into our kitchen. Maybe I did it because he looked like a timid, lost, probably hungry child; therefore I was ready to share my scarce food with him. I was grateful the soldier brought me a letter from Stephan; I was going to read it in privacy. Although my Russian language skills were limited, the soldier understood me and gave every sign of being relieved to be invited into a home.

Not only was our space rationed, but so were our provisions. I was barely earning enough to buy basic food that kept us from starving. I constantly searched for temporary work opportunities like whitewashing apartments, repairing broken furniture, and sewing dresses for women who had the cloth but could not afford a professional seamstress. Mother's culinary inventiveness flourished even when the ingredients were scarce. Each day, my mother somehow managed to create a new soup that kept us going. I was always hungry, dashing here and there to keep up with my commitments while looking for steadier employment. I wanted to make up for my lost school years but had to find the means to do so.

In some languages "a good soup" has a double meaning. The nourishment expresses more than just satisfying the needy stomach at the most basic level. I remember learning that in French *une bonne soupe* alludes to the attributes of a beautiful woman, indicating her abundant assets. I understood this sumptuously satisfying explanation as a compliment to describe sexually attractive women.

In German the saying—"to be in the soup" (*Ich bin in der Suppe*)—means to be in trouble. The German broth is a rather plain potato soup, nourishing but not really memorable or something to cherish. A potato soup asks for imagination. It is possible of course that the idiomatic imagery for the German male population might have started with tasting the splendors of cooking by French women who were neighbors. As culinary discoveries increased, the saying turned into a proverb. Through the ages, the constantly shifting borders and blurred political alliances are sometimes hidden in the creative folk art of ceramics, embroideries, and sayings.

My own curiosity to find logical meaning in words probably started when I, like most Jewish children, first learned Hebrew. In the onomatopoeic ancient language deriving from nature's sounds and logic, the color red is *adom*. *Daam* is blood, *adama* is soil. Adam, the first man, was created from the earth. To me, this sounded like the echo of his heartbeat, pumping life fluid through veins and arteries and reminding me of the circulation of memories flowing through the streams of conscious existence.

Mother's soup was a one-dish meal even when the meat was of lesser quality or entirely absent. For taste and some color and substance, she would add tomatoes or onion cut in half roasting it with the skin to medium brown in a skillet or open fire. This added aroma as well. It was of course difficult to identify all the ingredients as the shapes sometimes simmered into unrecognizable form, but the flavors were magnificent. All kind of roots were nourishing and tasty, like carrots and parsnips, celery, parsley, leeks, potatoes. Anything that our meager budget could buy went into mother's soup pot, with a few beans already soaked and cooked. If we had some oil or fat, onions and finely chopped garlic would be fried with flour and as a thickener added to the hot soup. That of course often made the difference between hot water and soft roots, or a tasty satisfying meal.

Before the war, my grandmother was legendary for her culinary innovations. Paula, our live-in maid, was a good cook too. Mother started her culinary experiments at a time when most basic ingredients were out of her reach, yet her talent and eagerness were obvious. She would not give up trying to put a warm meal into my bowl. I never complained as it was up to me to earn enough for rent and to pay for my schooling and all other expenses. The municipal taxes, electricity, and rent were essentials; food was a secondary necessity in our budget. Bread and fresh vegetables were of utmost importance to us. It took me many years to appreciate well-prepared food and allow it to represent a satisfying part of my life, rather than the indulgent luxury it was considered immediately after the war.

The soldier must have been homesick; I could sense it in his respectful behavior. Stephan's letter was still unopened in my pocket. The fact that Stephan wrote, and this unlikely messenger brought his letter, was gratifying.

We sat at the table with my mother's embroidered white tablecloth; its holes were beyond repair, and yet we used it and washed it with memories from another time. The irreparably torn linen tablecloth set off the delicate porcelain plates that rested on it. Another contradiction of war. We were using the fine china because we had sold our vintage stoneware; only plain sturdy plates were in demand.

My basic concern during the war was to have food on my plate. That need slowly subsided when I found my mother. By now I craved the kind of company we had before. I grew up with a beautiful family table that no longer existed. The image was sneaking up on me with memories of animated conversations at our expanded dining table. In childhood I was taught the significance of sharing a meal and hospitality, as well as interesting conversation. Now at a distance from that time, even a meager meal represented a source of life. All of us had learned that profound lesson. Mother, the soldier, and I were sitting at the kitchen table during a war but sharing a moment of tranquility.

It is not easy to share anything with a stranger, especially food if you have been undernourished for a long time. I really wanted to show my own hospitality to the soldier who brought a letter from Stephan. But how could I, with my limited Russian? How could I in any language, since my years of silence on the farm had left me hesitant to express myself? At the end of the war, I had to relearn even the simplest conversation in all the languages in which I had been fluent. Silence is only comfortable if one has experienced long-lasting isolation.

The three of us were slowly spooning our meal. The soldier was crying soundlessly, tears dropping into his plate. Salt was a rare commodity and my mother was using it sparingly, yet that young man's tears were not falling into his soup to add flavor. Mother and I did not look at his deep distress. We had learned to offer privacy to others' feelings by making ourselves invisible, not intruding—this is the one comfort we are always capable of giving another person. We did not need to be witnesses to his profound pain.

A bowl of soup with bread can be a substitute for a five-course dinner. Silence can be a substitute for conversation. I never asked questions if someone did not offer information, as I never knew what to do with lies. I feel grateful to have been taught to trust. Words sound like the vibrating tone of a musical instrument. A lie sounds like hitting a flat note. It is out of tune. Confronting reality, of course I experienced deceptions and lies. Imposture, even treachery, were valuable lessons, and I paid the price for learning. There are always experts around, eager and ready to satisfy our needs to help us in our self-deceptions. I learned the importance of silently maintaining the clarity of what I believed was true.

I did not want to ask the soldier about the ferocity of the battles he fought, how far away he was from his home, or if his home still existed. Such facts were relevant only to him. The reality we shared at that long moment was the difficulty he had in locating me, and then his effort to deliver the letter. Perhaps just as difficult was my invitation that reciprocated his effort. The entire scene of a meal around a kitchen table could have conjured up a long-lost image for the soldier of his own home. I only thought about the blood-smeared envelope of the letter. Mud overlay the stale red smear. This soldier came to be a messenger for the man with whom I shared a brief romantic dream. Someone with whom I had thought, even for a short time, I might share my future. I even thought of accompanying Stephan on that very journey from where he probably had written that letter.

When Stephan and I met just months earlier, the attraction had been mutual and very instantaneous. There had been so much death around me for years, and there was Stephan, so alive and strong. At nineteen I felt neither. I believed that I must have represented some kind of symbolic fantasy for Stephan, a Jewish girl, one he dreamt about. After all, he had not seen any girl up close for a long time. I first met Stephan and Martin when they bravely and ingeniously managed to convince a military medical unit to take the barely alive young Jewish men from the Nazi forced labor camp in southern Serbia in the copper mines of Bor to our Jewish community center in Belgrade. Stephan and Martin were in a way the healthiest and strongest of the survivors. The copper mines of Bor were a notoriously deadly place. Young Jewish men from Eastern Europe were forced to work there until they died. When the German Army hurriedly withdrew from the region, they left the remaining prisoners, who were barely alive, to starve to death.

In the power vacuum, the advancing partisans looked for weapons and food, not for emaciated, dying Jewish slave-labor survivors too weakened for combat. Help was far and slow. Peasants of the surrounding region of Bor were zealously guarding their meager food supplies from any marauders who intruded into their impoverished farms. They would shoot to kill anyone who approached their property, especially unarmed and weakened starving prisoners like Stephan and Martin, who raided the chicken coops and stole anything they could catch and silence with their bare hands. The prisoners were not just looking for themselves. What they did was to feed those still able to eat while they also tended to the dying and the makeshift burying of those who were already dead. We heard all this from the few men who could talk about their ordeal after they came to us from Bor. The Red Cross had brought the survivors to Belgrade and then to us because they were Jews and foreigners. We were the first station to receive those who still desperately hung on to life.

This was where Stephan's needs and my own meshed into a brief relationship. Years of fears, deprivations, the random luck of surviving the isolation, then changed to what was an abundance of hopes, a relationship with a real person that before was only a dream. Every day Stephan, Martin, and I worked together and then they escorted me home, where we had a meal together. Within the deadly currents of the immediate post occupation, which was slow to establish order and basic laws, I felt very secure with my tall and strong bodyguards. The three of us established a beautiful island of friendship and trust. We were survivors, and so we did not have to talk much in order to understand each other.

At the time, I had been a volunteer, taking care of the injured and hopelessly ill friends of Stephan and Martin. This was work at which I couldn't possibly succeed. In spite of trying, I felt desperate about my ignorance of what to do and our makeshift hospital, with even the most basic painkillers lacking. All I could do was hold the hand of the desolate, weak, often dying young men. Regardless of how poorly equipped, the infirmary was the urgent first stop and, for some, the injured and the weakened young men, their only destination.

We prepared our precious survivors for their additional journey, as the International Red Cross had accepted them for its convoy north to Hungary, Rumania, and mostly to Slovakia. We were gathering blankets and whatever food rations we could for the additional journey. Stephan and Martin tried to convince me, and everyone organizing the convoy, how important it was that I accompany them as additional help. Had I gone I probably would have been killed. It is amazing how self-preservation is mobilized in perilous times. My decision to stay had nothing to do with my concern about leaving my mother alone. It had less to do with the chief rabbi, Dr. Alcalay, insisting that I was needed at my work. My priority must have been outlined in some space in my preconscious. I must have been clinging to the life I had before it had turned into chaos. After all, I was already trying to re-create that blissful past by reconstructing it in my immediate plans. I was definitely going to continue my education to build my life and become my own person. This may be a simple dream we all share. I would not give up my goal for a romantic fling that burned very brightly because of all the darkness around us. But I knew the real reason was my fear of war in this new version of war's chaos. It was out of sheer fear that I did not join my friends.

I SAT ACROSS from the Russian soldier whose tearful face was like that of a child in pain. I did not want to know what he had or hadn't done when the battlefield might have placed him in a trance. None of us who have ever faced real terror has the need to uncover someone else's protective skin, to make one emotionally strip and show the raw wounds we hope will heal into scars. This is the respect we can offer someone, in not exposing the person's inner cover of integrity.

After we sat in silence at the table for some time, I felt I had to read the letter, written half in Slovak and half in Serbian. I realized that the words Stephan had chosen were in the language in which he knew I would understand his feelings for me. It was a beautiful love letter, filled with hopes for a reunion.

After his grim reality in the labor camp saturated with death, despite the short span of our knowing each other, Stephan Kroh did not see me as a romantic fling or daydream. His words were like a sparkling firework expressing the beauty of the flare that was love. His words became an anchor for me and I reread that letter for years. I knew it by heart.

WHEN THE RUSSIAN soldier was leaving, I asked him if Stephan Kroh was dead. Yes he was, the soldier said, looking relieved that I didn't ask more. At the door he thanked me for our hospitality; his voice was barely audible.

MORE THAN HALF a century has passed and here I am, attending conferences of survivors from the Holocaust. At all those gatherings there is a large bulletin board on which we write names of people we search for and about whom we hope someone might have information. Some of us put up enlarged faded photographs in case one might recognize a familiar face from the past. We always include our personal addresses.

Each year at those conferences I write the names: Stephan Kroh and Martin Goldberg. Maybe our young men were killed in battles on the road, maybe by the neighbors when they arrived home. We never received information about the fate of our transport. The journey had started at Bor and crossed through our Jewish community center in Belgrade. We were the halfway station on their journey.

It is my need to write again and again the names of my friends no one is looking for. I am writing their names because their existence remains very much alive within my memory. They are and always will be part of my youth before they had left on their homebound route, the journey I did not join.

I AM STILL grateful to the soldier who brought me Stephan's letter.

it was good of you incidental stranger

to send your legacy in the message

after our dreamlike togetherness

the words created a soft pillow

for my weary head

being awake

Soap Bubbles

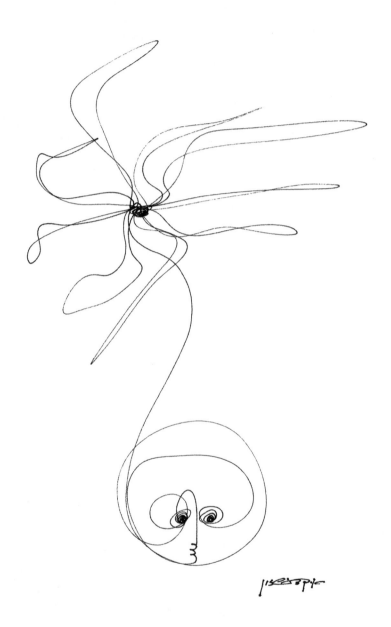

floating within the air

showing the entire rainbow color range

a soap bubble

arouses a strange urge to catch

the splendor

although it will rupture at the touch

like an emotion resisting capture

The scent of freshly washed laundry has always furthered my well-being. My earliest memories and sensations of feeling well were connected to water. The smell of clean water, freshly washed linen, the scent of a particular fragrance inside a bar of soap could trigger images in my brain out of a very distant time. Multiple events could line up in my memory, starting a spin, and connecting events from long ago, surprising me, as if finding an old photograph stashed in an unlikely place.

Laundry days were fun when I was a child because of Nelly Gatter who was hired for the monthly wash. At that time the washing was done by hand, with washboards, brushes, and big kettles where all those large sheets, pillowcases, and towels had to fit in and boil. I liked the sound burping bubbles created; boiling water was like a live, exhaling creature.

Those large cauldrons were sitting on short-legged iron wood-burning furnaces whose long pipes reached into the open air courtyard belching out smoke. Washing and boiling were taking place in the covered entrance behind our main gate. Most dwellings I was familiar with had gates leading into a covered entrance. That space usually led towards a yard and garden. We had a door leading into our living quarters. There was another door to the kitchen from the yard, close to the uncovered entranceway. There was a small cottage at the end of the garden where our maid Paula and her husband lived. In rainy weather the covered space beyond the gate provided our playground. The large gate was not opened as we did not have a horse and carriage.

There was an ordinary door that was usually locked, so our play domain was secure. On laundry days that semi-closed space created a commotion through the entire household. All that excitement was entertaining for my sister Susan and me, watching people working and arguing, and Nelly conducting the show.

We liked Nelly because she was different from the women who were hired for special work. Before holidays there was a lot of baking and extra cooking in our household; thus besides Paula our maid, our Grandmother had outside helpers. There were the expert noodle makers, fruit preservers, and the tomato juice preservers for the long seasons where neither fresh fruit nor tomatoes were on the market.

We all loved tomato soups, so there had to be a way to preserve a large amount of the precious liquid until the coming summer. Bottles and glass containers were boiled to make them sterile for preservation. Then the produce was prepared with additional boiling to avoid spoiling. The bottles were sealed with goatskin parchment that was boiled to make it kosher. The softened goatskin was stretched over the filled bottles to seal them. Cooling and drying turned the parchment seal into a smooth stiff surface as on a drum. I particularly enjoyed watching this process. There was a lot of labor invested in having tasty and healthy food on the table. The basic well-being of being clean was a lengthy tedious procedure as well.

Laundry soap was also made at home. The yearly supply was prepared in the yard because of the boiling ingredients' fumes and odors, which were rather unpleasant. The thickened soap brew was poured into wooden molds to harden and cut into squares after drying for a couple of days. That procedure stopped after kosher laundry soap became available.

For us girls it was obvious that Nelly was a lady as she was treated that way by our parents and grandmother. Nelly would sit at our dining room table, joining our meals, and involved in our conversations during meals as a guest would be. My older sister Susan and I were already aware about social difference in our society, the status and rules in interactions and the places in which one was supposed to fit. We learned there were rules and behavior patterns around eating at the table. Nelly was our equal; that was obvious from her exquisite table manners. Her whole bearing showed quality. Her language was that of an educated person. At that time in the 1930s her work was washing the laundry of other people, which was difficult, but she was a lady we were firmly told. In spite of her swollen hands from excessive hot water, soap, and strenuous washing and wringing, Nelly was very beautiful. I recognized that even as a small girl.

There are few people I remember with such clarity from my childhood. There are even fewer who had such an impact on my behavior as Nelly. I never forgot her.

Nelly considered us girls as growing ladies and not spoiled children. From early childhood Susan and I were taught to wash our own underwear as ladies are supposed to do. We related to washing. Because Nelly had her meals with us, Susan and I first thought that the reason for her presence was to introduce us girls to the superb table manners Nelly exhibited and that we should emulate her. We believed she was Jewish because there was a familiar relationship between our grandmother and Nelly, who seemed younger than Mother. Our curiosity led Grandmother to elaborate explanations, always starting with World War One, providing us with snippets of history just so we knew the contexts of time, place, and politics, all before answering our initial question. Grandmother, with her flair for connecting human behavior to historical events, goaded Susan and me to become ardent readers of history books. As Grandmother's lecture was about Nelly's past—which was intriguing to me, because her present somehow did not fit into the life patterns I understood—I listened carefully.

Nelly's husband was a ship's captain on the Danube waterways trade route between ports before and during the war of 1914 to 1918. At that time in the Austro-Hungarian Empire, my grandparents had a grain transporting business. Nelly's husband, the young Austrian Captain Gatter, was working with my grandparents who were grain merchants. At the end of the war, the defeated Austrian government did not want to reinstate the captain on their Danube fleet. He had worked with Jews. My grandparents lost all the money they had invested in the Kaiser Franz Joseph's war bonds. The captain lost his commission. As an Austrian he became unemployable in the newly created country of Yugoslavia as well. Due to the peace treaty in Versailles, Novi Sad, a significant port city on the Danube, became part of the new monarchies in the Balkans. The other was Albania.

Those were the realities of the war that was supposed to end all wars. Grandmother's disquieting comments about the lost family fortune were never mentioned before although we knew of it. Grandmother must have felt strongly about Captain Gatter and Nelly's present situation. Never before had I encountered people who were rejected and became outcasts on both sides of the same political conflict. I knew some of the Russian families who had escaped the Bolshevik Revolution and fled with their families to safety. They mostly belonged to the aristocracy or the high military ranks. Almost all were greatly impoverished but highly respected in the community. An Armenian congregation had also found refuge in our multifaceted Novi Sad, a city with a long historic memory.

SOME JEWISH REFUGEES started to arrive from central Europe in the mid-thirties, producing an undercurrent of unease in our Novi Sad Jewish community. This unease escalated to clear fear due to the reawakening of the old pattern of segregating minorities. First, young educated people recognized the increasing discriminations and began leaving their homes to escape a dangerous future. Established elders continued to live in denial. When the full impact of thoroughly organized hatred hit us Jews, few knew how to deal with a terror no one had imagined.

The war fell upon us in 1941, after two years of indulging in the self-deception that we would eventually be spared. I learned through experience how it felt to be utterly rejected, disregarded, nonexistent, invisible as a person. This all resulted in not belonging, living in a void even after the war was over.

It helped me to understand the meaning of being discarded through absolute discrimination. What had troubled me as a child about Nelly and her husband's fate began to become clear. Captain Gatter didn't go down commanding his sinking ship. His ship was just fine floating with another skipper. He was asphyxiated by political machinations on the firm ground of human disregard. On that centuries-old stage for political refugees, he was caught in the quicksand of the postwar tangle everyone avoids and from which there is no rescue. There is no welcome place for surviving nonentities.

Dead heroes can be mourned and turned into symbols, but what do we do with outcasts? Few people in any society seem ready to help the residue of doomed humanity, let alone open their doors and let them in. The handsome captain and his beautiful wife Nelly were sinking through the hourglass sands of the Danube dunes surrounding the shores of post–World War One Novi Sad.

YEARS EARLIER, IN the 1930s, I as a young girl wanted to see them as they had looked in the wedding picture Nelly had brought for us girls. They were the most beautiful couple I had ever seen in a wedding photograph. At the beginning of the century, when the photograph was taken, they looked like a fairy-tale couple, handsome, happy, almost majestic—she in a splendid gown with a lace collar showing her graceful long neck, he in a sparkling white uniform.

Childhood is such a wondrous bubble. I simply disregarded the shabby clothing they both were wearing in the present, her swollen hands, the graying, unruly, non-coiffured hair Nelly tied in a bun at the back. Her husband, equally downtrodden, was for me still that good-looking man with the flair of a ship's command and the air of fine manners he exhibited even toward us small girls. Of course both my sister and I had a crush on the captain. It did not matter to me that the only living the captain could make was to work as the exterminator of bedbugs in Novi Sad, while his beautiful bride was washing other people's dirty clothes. As the sense of fear began to spread all around in the world of adults, I didn't want to let go of the imagined splendor.

Europe was already rumbling with preparations for a new war. Political events had entered a high-speed dynamic, which generated a tension that was felt within our town's Jewish community. Nelly was still regularly arriving at our house to do the laundry, but she had lost her beautiful, self-confident posture. She was not well, Mother said. I believe Mother encouraged Nelly to tell Susan and me what was going on in her life. They were talking a lot.

Nelly was pregnant, Mother said, and under the circumstances and because of her age, they could not dare to have a baby. One of Nelly's regular workplaces was the home of a doctor who agreed to perform an abortion. Nelly would reimburse him with her work. We knew about the termination of pregnancies. One of our relatives had just concluded his medical studies. He clarified to Susan and me all those facts of life that were rarely properly explained to young girls. Our parents wanted us to be informed about the risks of sexual intercourse—of venereal infections, diseases, and pregnancies—so we were given lectures that informed us and probably diminished our curiosity about adolescent sex.

Equipped with such important information, I of course shared my knowledge with my friends, which created a buzz with my friends' indignant parents about my outrageous revelations. Of course I must have felt very superior having such knowledge. My parents were amused that the strongest outrage came from our family physician, who had ignorant daughters my age.

We all laughed and I thought no more about it until I heard Nelly's story. Because it was that same complaining physician who, before performing the medical procedure, insisted on having intercourse with her. Nelly greatly regretted that she had agreed to that humiliation. Nelly's revelation was upsetting to me. She stressed to Susan and me not to ever let that physician examine either of us without our mother being present. Such a situation never arose.

With its brewing war atmosphere, the late thirties were already shattering the moral and humanitarian codes of many people around us. In spite of my youth, Nelly's helplessness added to the uncertainties mounting around my own growing femininity. Fragments of these events remained as part of my prewar memory.

Soon after Nelly had confided to us her ordeal, her husband had a fatal accident while working to exterminate vermin. While activating the cyanide gas container, he apparently did not leave himself enough time to get out of the otherwise sealed apartment. The rule was that only one door was hermetically taped from the outside. The captain died from inhaling the poisonous gas. For our family this was a tragic accident. There were nasty comments, assuming that the captain was so drunk that he couldn't find the exit door. What is unclear in my recollection is how soon after her husband died that Nelly became very ill, was hospitalized, and died as well.

NELLY REMAINED VERY much alive within my memory. Not only through the four years of war that followed as I turned fifteen. I was on my own and alone. In 1941 my adolescent mind had to absorb the Nazi onslaught on Yugoslavia, turning Serbia into chaos. Fortunately I did not yet entirely comprehend the severity of the whole tragedy. The berserk Nazi ideology triggered that mega-slaughter. The murder of us Jews became the Reich's absolute central obsessive goal. I was still in the blessed enveloping bubble of partial maturity, where adolescence finds imaginative enclaves that create a secluded respite from reality. The impact of my abruptly changed life did not immediately freeze me into the inaction in which more mature people were caught. Instead of completely immobilizing my energy, my initial fear of the invader churned my defiance into a persistent physical strength that surprised me. I am not sure if I really grasped the reality of mortal danger if I were to be caught. Being an outlawed teenager, my life depended entirely on random chance and the goodwill of strangers. Fear was at times gripping my guts. Yet my adolescent fantasy was allowing me the sliver of invincibility and escape, the helpful bubble of occasional daydreams.

DURING THE FOUR years hiding during the Nazi occupation, one of my tasks was doing the laundry of the farmers who gave me shelter. Nelly often appeared in my mind. I learned to saw logs, chop wood with a hatchet, make a fire, lift a heavy kettle, scrub clothes with a wash board, wring heavy cloth and with pegs secure them on a rope, at times in harsh weather. The hard frozen winters were difficult times for laundry. I had to gather all my angry energy for the task, not to admit that a city-bred girl was incapable of heavy work. Nelly did it.

This was a farm. Brushing the mud from clothing before washing it was only additional labor. But I was not forgetting who I was or the different world I came from. During that time, my mind was rarely focused to allow me to comprehend events, to order them cohesively or even with clarity. I just knew it was important not to view myself as a powerless farmhand, washing a stranger's soiled clothing. This was what I did in hiding to stay alive, secluded from a world where death reigned. As much as the ordeals were painfully difficult, I was alive. This harsh war was temporary.

I frequently remembered Nelly during those years. She helped me to hold on to who I was, who I would be if I survived the no-man's-land of absolute rejection. I was young enough to convince myself that ahead of me there was a promised land if I would survive the war.

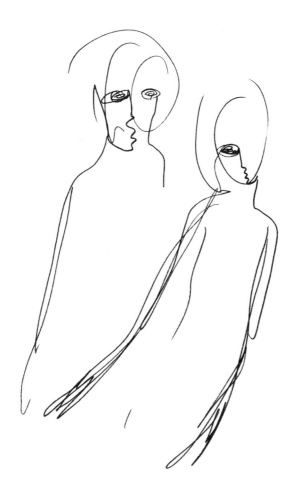

Hidden beyond Mountains

I was given abundance to toy with

love choices confidence

to toss them all into the air and juggle

through ravaging experiences

to mostly struggle or with flare create resilience

to develop imagination from the need to compensate

for lack of response or an echo

to rebound in that vast land of rejection

where inner rocks grind hopes

and distrust erupts

in a scorching lava flow

eventually

molten rocks form fertile grounds

furthering growth

"It is there beyond those mountains. That lake is so large that they say if you stand on the shore you don't see where it ends. Have you already been there?" She looked at me eagerly. Her expression was that of a child waiting to hear again what she already knew, Lake Ochrid's vast size and beauty. She seemed pleased when I said I had never even been near the lake.

I was a guest in this splendid mansion, a palace, home of the mayor of this small town in the south of Yugoslavia. For the town's highest official the arrival of the exploratory documentary film crew was an exciting change in the postwar Communist era. Exhibiting his deference to the government, the hospitality of opening his home to a government run project, the mayor showed strong interest in a cultural activity that would extend the prestige of this remote area, different in time and customs.

I was part of that elite scouting film crew. I belonged to a different world. The young woman talking to me was curious about me because to her I probably represented some kind of government power. She wanted to know if I had a gun, and seemed disappointed when I said I didn't care to own one. Samia lived in a palace with servants and luxuries. I sensed that to her my presence was an erratic enjoyment, yet disturbing at the same time.

We were in the southeastern part of Yugoslavia, close to the Albanian and Greek mountainous regions with their Moslem minorities. Although I lacked experience, I was awarded that lucrative assignment because I studied theater set, interior architecture, and costume design and because I was a woman.

Samia appeared pleased when I said that I had never been at the lake either. We at least shared something unfulfilled. The young woman spoke so wistfully about Lake Ochrid that I felt relieved that we had postponed our visit. It took a couple of hours to get to the lake from her village. Her melancholy repetition about the lake seemed ridiculous to me. I did not care nor did I understand enough to recognize the allegory she was attempting to construct. She might have been sheltered from the war, which had ravaged her surroundings. Her perception of the world was a blurred fantasy, not reality. She was probably younger than I. While I was engaged sketching ornaments, furniture, embroidery patterns, and adornments for our film project, the girl was watching me. She hesitantly tried to engage me in conversation, speaking a fluent Serbian, but did not ask about my past. Apparently our hosts knew that I belonged to the Jewish minority hunted by the Nazis, and that I had to hide with strangers for four years. Maybe for Samia my past was a fantastic romantic adventure.

I remained in my remote comfort of not interacting. I was used to not communicating. Nevertheless I remember I felt sorry for the girl, although at the same time it seemed ridiculous for me to pity someone who lived in such lavish, well-protected affluence. Yet I knew that I reacted superficially, even callously, toward that girl's need to reach out. I was still in my own shelter, a hardened cocoon.

At the beginning of 1948 I was cautiously balancing a painful recent past with my mounting doubts and present political dissatisfaction. I did not fit within this totalitarian state and there was no legitimate way to go anywhere. I was mainly concentrating on acquiring a profession I liked, and allowing myself occasional daydreams. At that location I was admiring and documenting Islamic art of centuries applied to daily objects, the wealth of a culture that had been in the area for five hundred years.

The planned documentary film was to feature this remote region, and therefore we wanted to continue on and cross Albania to reach the capital, Tirana, on the Adriatic. Besides me, our crew consisted of the director, the cameraman, and the producer, who was obviously a political commissar. Zika the director told me he had requested that I be part of the crew because he respected my work at the studio in Belgrade, and he was convinced that I would bring a sensitivity in dealing with minorities addressed by the documentary. I liked the compliment but was aware that I was given the assignment because I knew how to accurately sketch and then build what was required and as a woman I could enter the women's quarters.

Our cameraman was a creative photographer. He was probably in his forties and I considered him an old lecher because girls passing him in the Belgrade studio corridors would usually get a pat on their backsides. When he did it to me, I punched him. His swollen face looked pathetic. After that incident he exhibited a respectful and somewhat guarded behavior toward me.

The producer for our project was a new addition to the studio. I was particularly careful in my attitude toward him. No one would mention his political background in the production, but the fact was clear. He organized all the logistical details efficiently and with a relaxed firmness that emanated from his elite position. Throughout the project, he would enter any civilian or military office and quickly provide whatever we needed in material or human help. Since I had so much experience with bureaucratic slow motion, I recognized real power at work.

JUST AS I promised, I never sketched any of the women's faces. Yet I did not forget Samia's enigmatic expressions as she watched me. Hesitantly, she attempted to ask oblique questions of how I worked with the strange men in the film industry. I was glad to have been busy all the time, as she seemed almost hungry listening to my mostly technical answers. She spoke Serbian fluently but I was too deeply involved in my work to realize what she really tried to express in her wistful talk. She repeatedly spoke about traveling beyond the mountains surrounding her hometown. As I was about to leave with our film crew, Samia said she hoped to see Lake Ochrid some day.

Soon after we left that location, I realized that my thinking about Samia lacked objectivity and that I was shortsighted in my views. We were both young, spoke the same language, yet we remained within our complexity, light-years apart.

DURING THAT PERIOD I still felt the chaos of war under my skin. Rationally I tried to crawl out of my hiding by moving ahead cautiously and with distrust toward authorities while painfully realizing how we Jews had almost become extinct in Europe. During the war I had functioned primarily in an intuitive state of basic existence without the luxury of time to logically think and analyze events, or understand people's behavior. Constant vigilance was part of me. I lived in complete freedom, a jungle animal. Later on I realized how comparing my trust of my worldliness with Samia's experiences was naive and immature. Samia was also a veteran, but of sheltered restrictions and restraint. The comfortable cage of her entire existence was protecting her from external injuries, but it stifled her needs of expanding her eventual capabilities beyond zealously prescribed rules.

This young woman's life was entirely planned and controlled. I was utterly ignorant about what that meant. I was free to decide and move according to my abilities. I lived, worked, and traveled with strangers.

When we parted, it was obvious we would not meet again. Samia wistfully said she envied me, and in my lingering immaturity due to years of growing in isolation from a normally developing life, I did not understand what she tried to convey.

BEFORE WE ARRIVED at the border of Albania we were introduced to our driver who spoke Serbian with an accent. The young man with a pleasant smile was going to be our guide, translator, and mechanic on the journey. He drove a spacious open military vehicle with a machine gun mounted beside him. Our producer took the front seat next to the gun. Zika the director sat in the back between the cameraman and me. We crossed the border to Albania near the city of Peshkopia. It was a familiar name. In Serbia, if you wanted to be moderately crude and curse someone, you'd say, "go to Peshkopia." The local swear words were both more elaborate and bluntly visceral.

In the early morning hours we descended from the high mountains to the valley, which looked like a sunken crater. Soon we developed an inkling of what hell was supposed to be like. In spite of the open military vehicle offering the benefit of a breeze, breathing became an effort. Farther downhill, as though emerging out of a furnace, we were hit by hot air. We were moving, but the intense heat was like a sparkling liquid mass quivering around us. We cut through it. When we reached the valley, the air was scorching and motionless. Like a choking blanket thrown over me, it was frighteningly incapacitating. Even early in the day this place was punishing. Our driver slowed down because we were passing through what was probably the main street in Peshkopia. I sustained an experience which became part of the horrifying pile of images that was already engraved in my brain.

A group of men in single file, connected by a chain, was slowly dragging itself to seemingly nowhere. Each man carried a shackle with a chain ending in an iron ball. The entire body had to carry itself while pulling an additional dead weight. I thought my mind had played a trick on me. This could not be real; this looked like a scene out of the middle ages, or a pre-Renaissance apocalyptic nightmarish vision!

We had just fought and defeated unimaginable cruelties, but did we really? I had seen what the Nazis had documented on films left behind by the German Army as they withdrew. Images of horror beyond imagination. Where were we in the process of evolution?

I looked at a man who probably heard our approaching car in the silence as there was no other traffic. He abruptly stopped to move, lifting his head. I looked at the man. I remember his face, his dark-blue eyes that lit up, became radiant, and brightened his entire expression with delight, a young man's face looking at a girl. As fast as his face flared into a spark of joy, it quickly turned into despair at his doomed reality. I witnessed that instantaneous horrifying transformation. I became part of that dramatic change and it took my breath away. It was not the heat hitting my lungs; it was the pain that hit my brain. It was an instant that for me has lasted through my lifetime. Maybe it had the same effect on that young man; only his time was counted on a different cosmic clock.

I DON'T KNOW how many seconds it took to experience that encounter, since we were moving in different directions. I felt as I did in the heavy bombardments during the war after hearing the unmistakable whistling, screeching sounds of falling bombs, and learned to count seconds from the sound till the blast of the explosion. It was the time that indicated the distance of someone's agony or death. At that time I knew there was some reprieve from my immediate doom. Silence became the dread of the unknown fear that can never be measured; maybe fears are timeless.

WHAT I NEVER experienced was imprisonment. During the war I was like a hunted animal, alive, hiding from the searching predators, aware, on constant watch, and not even trusting the illusory security of my shelter in the changed perilous chaos of war. But I was never deprived of that most elemental, natural need to move freely, as I was never caught and forcibly immobilized. What I had witnessed in Peshkopia was beyond recorded documentations or what I had seen in films or heard from witnesses. As we looked at each other, I became a witness to a timeless bond, connecting to horror beyond escape.

THE DRIVER WAS accelerating toward our destination. The prisoners were already disappearing into a row of discarded human beings, the useless residue war leaves in its wake. That incident only took seconds but I remained devastated. For the last several years I had no tears left; now they were running down my face. Our producer must have seen what took place and noticed my reaction. "Those are vile criminals; do not feel sorry for them. They are in work camps to rebuild the country they destroyed," he said.

I am a coward. That is why I did not reply, "This is an Italian prisoner of war; his face is like one cut out from a painting in the Italian Renaissance, or Roman or Etruscan mosaics! Look at him! What are you talking about!" But I had learned a profound lesson during the war, even in pain. I knew how to stay mute, practically invisible. I drew away from Zika who was sitting beside me. I didn't want to talk, as we continued to distance ourselves from the horror, steadily climbing out of the valley heat. I had to avoid my emotions and start to think. But my thoughts were racing the way my emotions were. The recent parting from Samia who remained in her prison of embroidered pillows and lace curtains appeared in my mind. A young woman desperate to move freely. Usually thinking would distract me from emotional distress. This time my familiar practice did not ameliorate my upset. It compounded my impotence to influence even myself. The man condemned to chains, a soldier, a war prisoner, caught in the wrong place within the web of politics whose structure he could never understand. And here was I, who randomly survived the deadly dragnet. I had already started to rebuild my life without understanding its intricacy either. How did I express my active opposition right now? I remained silent.

I was traveling on the road that this chained young man might have built. But he will never enjoy traveling it. His face will remain familiar to me just as it was in that snap of time when it froze, imprinted in my own recognition of bearing witness, remembering and recording.

I recorded that incident in my art when I began to paint superimposed images. I would create depth, not through perspective, but as if constructing a double exposure on a flat surface, blending different images into each other. I was painting the memory of events and space as my emotional reactions to events. That memory is clustered on canvas or paper.

As our journey toward Tirana continued, my mind sped toward past experiences where I had witnessed cruelties I was incapable of influencing or changing in any way. Those paintings reminded me of my own limitations.

What part of my character was lost if I became lost in fear or hate or in my ever present insecure decisions? Could I end up turning into a perpetrator I so deeply despised? Or did I shrink into a cautious passive bystander, frozen into submission? How strong was my rational thinking when my self-control dropped away and all that was left was naked self-preservation? Would I ever dare to confront myself objectively? Could I begin to answer those questions that were constantly piling higher and higher? But if I do not clarify the mountains of growing hurt, doubts, fears, and frustrations about my own passivity, the disappointments in myself may turn to anger and build a mountainous fortress. Like a mental Tower of Babel, making it impossible to understand my diverse emotions, they will become a scrambled din. Or complete silence may take over and wither my mind into a desert.

ONCE OUT OF Peshkopia and the lowlands, I forced myself to concentrate on the winding road climbing the mountains. I could not afford tears right now. During my years in hiding, I used to escape into nature, which became my sanctuary. Looking at this alien landscape inhaling cool air as we drove higher was a relief. My thoughts turned to the landscape's color and shapes. Images of nature were my short time escapes when faced with emotional upheavals I didn't know how to deal with. The recent event brought out my insurmountable sorrows and loss, the war years. I was holding on to that past because I was not sure what else existed in me; or if I could move away from it—ever?

IN EARLY CHILDHOOD I recognized that observing my surroundings produced gratification. At first it satisfied my curiosity; later on it became entertaining. I could draw and paint from memory what I liked. During my teenage years in wartime my brief escapes to the tranquility of the woods improved my inner balance within a harsh present. Nature always inspired my daydreaming. Imagination improved how I felt. Occasionally I could will myself physically and emotionally to overcome incidents when the only resource to lift my spirit was my will.

WE WERE WARNED about marauders and bandits in the country. I decided not to think about the dark, dense, wooded sides of the road and instead enjoy the road, and what a road! Triangular rocks of the mountain peaks looked like the vertebrae of primordial dragons. It was easy to imagine those giants still roaming the earth right here. The forest seemed to move menacingly, encroaching on the road, conjuring in my mind the final scene in Macbeth. Here nature looked like appropriate scenery for any drama. I realized my past mental exercise was still functioning.

The winding road turned to rock formations where water and wind carved the stone, as if row upon row of sharp spears of an invisible army stood on guard. Here and there isolated stony spikes reached upward like rams. Protruding slabs hung over the road, as extended roofs. The view from the edge of the road, close to where I sat, was intimidating. It seemed as if part of the mountain abruptly slid into an abyss. The scenery looked, smelled, even sounded wild. I heard strange bird calls but never glimpsed the caller. Maybe in this wilderness once an animal was seen it was a dead one. The only visible birds were enormous eagles sitting on the edge of the road like spectators in the front row balcony waiting for a show. With no traffic the birds did not pay attention to our approaching car. We came pretty close before they took off, gliding elegantly above the vast emptiness. A confident predator is in no hurry. He owns the place.

Never before had I seen so many eagles. Floating on wondrous wide wings, suspended in the air, hovering above the valley. Some of the birds flew with their bounty dangling in their claws. Death in nature was for me a matter of the cycle of life. It was not the horror of wasteful, wanton, human killing when the reasons for wartime tragedy remained dubious.

In the distance, goats were visible on the craggy rocks. We did not see any bears. Our guide warned us to be careful and not to venture far from the car when we stopped to enter the dense vegetation that occasionally spilled onto the road. What had caught my attention was the scarcity of human settlements in the distant but visible valleys. This was an isolated country of solitary people living in uninhabitable hostile terrain. The Shiftars, as the Albanians were called, were supposed to be the ancient dwellers of the Balkan Peninsula. They could have been the descendants of the tribes depicted in Homer's *Iliad*. Supposedly written in the eighth century B.C.E., Homer's epic poems were inspired by the legendary oral history shrouding the area.

Throughout the centuries most invaders chose easier routes to expand their conquests; thus this part of the peninsula remained in a temporal slumber. Traveling this strange land, my thoughts and observations derived from snippets of literature and my personal curiosity. This road was built in the tradition of the ancient Romans, those masters of durable constructions. Like its forebears, modern Italy had occupied Albania at the beginning of the Second World War. The Italians had left this perfectly built asphalt road, cut into the mountains of an otherwise impenetrable region. What all the other occupiers and invaders in that war left was utter devastation.

Traveling in a spacious military vehicle I felt comfortable because for sure this was the fastest and most secure way to traverse such a remote land. Only now and then did we see a few valleys between the rocks of this domain of the eagles and wild goats. Scattered occasionally were stone structures visible on tiny green patches. Because there were houses with no chimneys, I wondered if those structures were dwellings. I did not feel like talking to our guide or anyone else after we left Peshkopia; therefore I didn't ask.

I was comfortable in my silence. But the driver, determined to explain this strange country, was telling me that most houses on those farms were constructed with no chimneys. During the entire day I saw very few of those strange dwellings. There were even fewer people visible in the rare and small cultivated patches of land.

We could see women working in the fields. They were carrying large baskets on their heads or strapped on like backpacks. There were smaller figures around which I first thought were children, but soon realized were short, bearded men. They seemed like pint-size inspectors just moving here and there. Since all the women I saw were so much taller than the men who accompanied them, I wondered if large women were chosen because that was the criteria of feminine beauty here or a preference derived from their ability to do physically demanding labor.

Perhaps this was an example of natural selection, of why they proliferate, like the Galapagos finches. In comparison, men who did not share the physical hardships may have turned shorter through generations. Of course this was my very personal view, but it intrigued me then and occasionally later.

THE SPELL OF pristine wilderness and my own meandering thoughts about Albania were suddenly changed as we reached Tirana at dusk. We were entering civilization. My quiet companions started to talk, maybe stimulated by what our driver said, that a night on that road could be dangerous. The driver looked relieved and with a big smile he said that on our way back he promised we would travel in a convoy. We had been fortunate that no incident had occurred on our journey. We had not encountered even one other car during the entire day. We carried additional cans of gasoline but that was what might have made us into a lucrative target, he said. We thanked our excellent driver who contributed to our good luck, keeping us moving through a country that never lacked plunderers who would ambush travelers.

Entering Tirana, a city with streetlights and smells of piled garbage, meant population, but the only pedestrians were armed soldiers. Paradoxically they were a comfort. I was still reacting to the events of the day, and its extraordinary sights of wilderness. But the day was over, and the hotel where we were to stay for the next few days looked very European. The occupiers had built this city for their own comfort and needs. For me the hotel felt like prewar luxury.

After a good dinner and wine, our entire crew became more agreeable. I was looking forward to sleeping in the impersonal hotel room. This would be different from my stay with Samia in the women's enclave with its entrapped aura. Reality started to feel more tidy and orderly, blurring the recent events. I had to stop my emotional responses to the journey from interfering with my work.

I did not know how men behaved after a dangerous journey but the producer was telling crude jokes and I felt disappointed to be part of such an insensitive group, especially because they were a creative team I had been proud to join. I believed Zika was different but I was wrong.

AT THE ONSET of our trip we all met at the Belgrade train station. All my companions carried suitcases. I had my belongings in three canvas bags. I did not own a suitcase nor could I buy one at that time. My earnings had different priorities. My personal decision was to buy only what was absolutely important or necessary and I was not going to explain my reasons. At that time no one shared personal thoughts since trust had become extremely rare.

When I noticed them smiling at my canvas bags, I told them that one contained my sketchbook and crayons for the assignment and the other two were just what I was going to wear and would simply throw away, as that was what I did with everything I used. If they had planned to tease or laugh about me during the trip, I made it clear I had answers. There were no more remarks about me not having a suitcase.

For years during the war each evening I would wash what I wore during the day. My clothes were ragged but clean, as my skin would easily break out. Now I made my underwear and outerwear from new material. Since I could not afford a sewing machine, I stitched clothes by hand. But I felt confident and comfortable in my own creations. They were original and becoming. I never bought clothes in the shops as they were expensive and looked like dull uniforms.

Even though I tried I could not deceive myself. It was not entirely on impulse that I took a nightgown on this journey. It was more of a long fine silk dress, made to order years before the war by Grandmother, who prepared my sister's trousseau. Grandmother had ordered it, Mother salvaged it through the war, but my sister Susan never wore it. It was such a fine silk it took up no space. I missed my sister more than anyone else. I had confidence in her superiority in knowledge and abilities. Susan trusted my loyalty never to say what she told me in confidence.

Because the war abruptly distanced us, Susan and I used to construct word puzzles and would exchange them when we met. I used to make watercolor pictures, Susan and my mother would stitch petit-points. Our meetings were short-lasting, infrequent, but highly cherished. The length and intensity of the war greatly drained our optimistic outlook on life. Bouts of silence and distance did not diminish trust; they only intensified the base we shared. When Susan became involved with partisan forces at the end of the war, I dreaded the twofold danger for her life but knew I could not say or do anything to influence what was unfolding. She had made her decisions.

AFTER THE WAR I used to wear her silk nightgown when I really needed solace. It always wrapped around me in gentle comfort, like a generous hug. After a rather strenuously eventful day and the crude jokes, a long shower felt soothing. Running water over my head to a great extent restored my calm. The nightgown was cool and soft.

Upon entering my room, there on my night table, on the leftover bite of the dessert I had taken to my room to slowly enjoy, sat the biggest roach I imagined could exist. I did not scream, but I might have gasped loudly. I was not used to screaming but maybe I did—I was choked, startled. There was an instant knock on my door. Embarrassed to have caused commotion, I opened it.

Zika the director stood in the doorway. His appearance was so instantaneous, I wondered if he had been standing outside my door all along. He looked disturbed. He had heard me cry out, which alarmed him since he knew I would not raise my voice with no reason. He had taken the room next to mine because he wanted to be sure I would be all right during the night. We were in a country that was still lawless and just beginning to stabilize. During our travel he realized the grave hazards in the country. There was no other young woman except me in the entire hotel, he said. Here were only military men and our party.

What happened? Was there anything he could do for me? Zika was worried, he said. He was responsible for me being in this location. He apologized for the producer's inappropriate jokes. They made all of them look ridiculous. They did not know me, he continued. "All of us, even armed, were tense on that road." He added that I was the only one who enjoyed the wilderness, looking at nature, I was sightseeing. He looked at me puzzled. "You were fearless in dealing with hazards, not absorbed in worries. Even with our weapons we were nervous. You were the only one enjoying this country's wilderness." Zika blurted all that out in one breath. Indeed he looked flustered, confused, disconnected from his usual confident, calm, almost stiff composure. I found him warm and compassionate, the person I thought he was.

He had never looked at me that way before, befuddled yet with an urgency not to be misunderstood. He remained respectfully at the door, waiting for me to explain why I had raised my voice; his voice was barely audible. He said that he admired my courage and understood me. Suddenly I felt happy realizing that he didn't know I was not brave and that I didn't want him to understand me, to discover my insecurities. I wanted to remain free, and independent, even though I felt attracted to him. We knew each other for over a year, but we both kept our distance out of respect for our different individual work. The physical closeness to Zika during the lengthy train ride from Belgrade south to Skoplije had fortified what I believed was a mutual attraction, bringing us closer. I remember waking up in the train, days before, with my head on his shoulder, which must have been uncomfortable for him; yet he didn't even slightly move to wake me. He let me rest, not saying a word.

There was no reason for me to be startled by a roach, let alone cry out. I had lived on a farm with rats, with mice running around my shack when the dogs were not around. There were all kinds of wanted and unwanted creatures around me for the duration of the war. Spiders and wasps, mosquitoes, pesky flies and fleas, all the hungry crawlers and flyers in their given season of a rural surrounding. I never cried out for help, but simply dealt with unpleasant situations.

My reaction had revealed a profound shift from my usual behavior, that was clear. For the first time in years I wanted to need help and even felt relieved, realizing my unforeseen behavior. Allowing myself to react like any girl my age, to scream at the sight of a roach, suddenly felt right. I was no longer a veteran farmhand as I had been during the war. Hitting the roach with whatever was handy and throwing it out for the ants would have been routine for me. For years I not only hid my identity, but my gender as well. Now it felt liberating to be needy and to have someone help me. I felt gratified being a woman.

During my years in hiding, I had suppressed my development as a woman, in fear of attracting men. I was aware of the hazard of rape, walking alone through wooded rural areas. If I screamed now because of a roach, I was emerging from my former anxiety. It was a relief to see Zika standing at my door eager to help. Especially as he kept repeating, practically pleading that he wanted to be sure I was all right. I needed help, was my reply.

Immediately, standing in my silk nightgown, I knew what had made me cry out. My scream was intentional; I wanted Zika in my room. He killed the roach. It was not a dragon.

Embroidered Memory

wayfarer

staunch on the wing

unwavering through season's diversities

riding turbulent air surfing over sparkling sways

or gray churning gales

weathered feathered mariner

we pass each other's path now and then

within the archaic draw we follow

summoned

to cross distances to the site

where our own flocks started

a lifelong glide

About a hundred yards from the road that runs parallel to the seashore stood rows upon rows of tents. This was the main road heading southward from the Haifa port where we arrived a few days earlier. We were placed in Beth Lid, a former military camp on the slopes of the northwestern Carmel range. The mountains were different from those I was familiar with. It was more like a chain of connecting hills with parched shrubs and occasional scrawny trees. Colors and smells were unfamiliar. The entire place was an altogether novel and exciting experience for me.

It had been my choice to come and live here. This was the summer of 1949. The country where I was born and considered my home had turned into an alien hostile environment where I felt like an unwanted stranger. Arbitrary rules break us in or break us up, or if we are fortunate, we break out and away. Luckily I had that chance.

Now here was my new home in an army tent. My mother and I shared it with three other families. The tent was spacious and a surprisingly comfortable shelter from the glaring sun. There was a pleasant breeze if all the sidewalls were open. The shifting wind came from the Mediterranean, moist, smelling of tang, the drying seaweed hanging all over rocks at low tide. The early morning breeze brought spicy aromatic scents of dry vegetation, reminding me of herbs in the exotic food I was looking forward to. Our food rations in the camp included familiar green olives and I loved them, as they smelled like pine trees. And we had some vegetables, sour cream, and fruit. Most important was the daily fresh bread.

My past was stashed away in my mind as if in a safe deposit box. Since my arrival an inner calm had swept over me. My tranquility was paradoxically unexpected. Everyone around the camp was generating anxiety about the future. It was not rational but I felt secure, as if my entire life would be devoid any problems. The basic change was sinking in.

Israel was a place prone to currents of international critiques, surrounded by angered enemy countries and unfriendly minorities within. This small stretch of land was rarely peaceful for any stretch of time in history. I craved peace. Yet I could not remember having been that calm and carefree. I felt unruffled for the first time since childhood but I could not explain that well-being.

Lying on a cot in a tent, open all around, listening to the night's hushed rustle of the nocturnal Carmel fauna, with occasional hoots, breathing in the humid sea air mixed with dry scents of an herbal bouquet, I was happy.

For our own security we were told not to leave the campground. Many years ago I stopped obeying any rules limiting my movements. A barbed wire fence was no hindrance either. Loving to swim I did not even try to resist the sparkle of the nearby shore surf. From the rocky beach I swam further west to get a wider view of the military camp. The hills stretched south, bathed in the afternoon sun. Looking north in the misty haze was the city of Haifa.

Leisurely swimming for about two hundred yards from the shore, I felt an undercurrent taking me south. I knew the energy of water from the Danube, and learned not to fight the power of a current. I was taught to drift for a while then angle my strokes diving toward the shore, then get to the surface for air and orientation. The rocks from where I started were already distant.

I knew I would have a lengthy walk back. The view of the hills alternated between barren edges of seemingly soft rock formations, where the rains had carved riverbeds. Dense vegetation was only near the water. It was a different scenery from the leafy forests of the continental climate I came from. This landscape told a story of harsh opposites. The merciless sun and flooding rain.

When I got out of the water, a narrow sandy stretch turned into soft muddy soil with reed-like plants. I grew up near the Danube with its swampy banks. I was familiar with the look of a similar vegetation whose roots hold the flooded ground. Being used to walk barefoot on coarse ground, the soft earth allowed me a fast pace to the paved road. I knew I had to reach the road leading to the camp before darkness. After sunset there was immediate darkness all around.

Reaching the road, I felt relief. There was a beautiful slanting sunlight on the hills which changed from a pale grayish green into a deep orange tint. A wide canyon divided two rounded hills on the opposite side of the road. On the northern hilltop were a number of houses.

That entire location is practically engraved in my memory. Those twin hills with a canyon between them. The southern lower rounded hill had an enormous gaping cave entrance. What I was looking at felt strangely familiar. It's possible that I saw a photograph of the location in a book during my childhood. This place did not seem to be noteworthy, neither religious nor cultural nor historical. Yet I almost recognized this place. Perhaps I had come across a photograph or drawing of this scenery in one of the books about the Holy Land that I had browsed through as a child. Yet through decades, whenever I traveled to Haifa from Tel Aviv and back, my sense of familiarity to that location never ceased.

There was a swampy lake around the southern Carmel area that had provided wild animals for the Hippodrome in the Roman Era, I later learned. That archeological site was just south from where the Carmel Range ended. The recently drained river that had spilled into the sea was called Nachal HaTa'aninim, the Crocodile River. I was told the entire area had recurring ground water. My new home started to connect me to distant history.

My recent history of the Second World War was simmering in my memories, unexpectedly creeping and expanding in my mind, within current events. Most people I knew did not want to talk or listen to experiences about that time; therefore I kept silent but I found through my drawings and paintings the means to describe my recollected evidence. I never perceived myself a victim; I survived that gargantuan mass murder because the Nazi force didn't catch me. Ever since, I have felt the obligation to testify what I know about that murderous hunt.

IN THE FIFTIES there was not yet a popular vocabulary to describe the shameful events of dehumanization. It took a passage of time for me to realize how the past was lingering on in my artistic expressions. I had entirely lost my singing voice and the bright colors in my paintings; before the war they were exuberant. Loss became a fact like other deprivations from the past I was integrating into my otherwise substantial present.

My present seemed to have an exceptional speed. Within one month upon arrival in Israel, I worked as the assistant set designer in the Cameri Theater in Tel Aviv, painting scenery, and designing costumes for current shows. I became engaged to be married, moved into an apartment. Most of the newcomers in mid 1949 were struggling in the transition to a new reality of place, some relearning our ancient resurrected language, finding work. I had the good fortune to find employment in my profession, and to meet Isaac, the organizing brain in that theater, who soon became my husband.

With that, my partner was highly aware and considerate of my needs for inner space. That was why we never had an argument. Isaac's logical ethic was that my mother living with us was my dowry, as she was going to be at home with our future children so I would be able to expand my creative abilities.

When life has such an unusual speed, our perceptions of time shrink. When we experience an overwhelming event, every detail becomes pertinent. Yet in retrospect, such events recoil.

IN THE SUMMER of 1949 I was painting in the courtyard of the theater. Passersby on the street could see me if they looked over the fence. As it was a time when many new citizens were looking for employment, some people would ask me if the theater needed workers. A group of newcomers from Yemen had settled in Tel Aviv. They were easy to recognize. They looked like the paintings by Abel Pan whose portraits of Yemenite Jews were highly popular in the Novi Sad Jewish community of my childhood. I easily recognized them. They wore different clothing, headdresses, jewelry. In Israel they represented a homogenous, very distinct group, utterly dissimilar from us, the European war survivors. In the Yemenite Jews I saw an image, as if looking into a time mirror that represented our traditions. While the raging persecution of Jewish Europeans continued, the Jews of Yemen had been isolated for hundreds of years.

There were restrictions and laws isolating minorities on the Arab Peninsula, rules prohibiting Jews from particular professions. After millennia of enforced adaptation of identity, we survivors had developed some characteristic differences. Now, we all shared our ancient tenacity to survive and the forever-present basic necessity to improve our once more forcibly changed reality in our historical birthplace.

One day, this urgency brought a middle-aged Yemeni man into the theater yard where I worked. He spoke the Hebrew I only partially understood from my childhood schooldays, learning the language of the Bible. But what I lacked in my language skills I recognized from experience in looking and finding work. When the man opened the bag he carried, I immediately put my paintbrush aside. It was a revelation for me to see the intricate design in silver adornments in that bag. He was a jeweler he said, who had his workshop in the Carmel Market and wanted to know if the theater needed jewelry. When I asked about the elaborate adornments, he said that he was dismantling the ancient jewelry and crafting earrings he could sell. He had in his bag the original traditional silver accessories. I was curious what was happening with the adornments unsuitable for earrings or brooches. All the silver would be sold for the price of the metal to be melted, was his answer. "We brought what we could carry like everyone does going away from where we were born. Our young women want to wear what is fashionable in Israel whether in clothing or jewelry."

THE MELTING OF these spectacular artifacts brought to mind the Nazi bonfires of books. I remembered the destruction of Jewish art culminating with the annihilation of Jewish lives in the not so distant past. This was present time, and we were in Israel, our home—all of us from different geographical and educational backgrounds, educated or with a lack of education due to the war, some of us with multiple capabilities or disabilities, but all of us trying to integrate, headlong to succeed and build a future.

I couldn't remain passive to the fact that the majority of Yemeni Jews were selling their treasured heritage, artistic tradition, their past. All of us survivors brought something we valued, could carry, and sell. We did not speak a common language yet. This man and I really had in common the appreciation of art when we saw it. He might have recognized it in my work, as I painted the backdrop of a fairy tale city on a large plywood cut-out that was part of the scenery I was working on.

Art, whether ancient or contemporary, has a profound impact on me. The theater had no use for that Yemeni art; but that day I started and continued to be an ardent collector. I had no idea what I was going to do with the items I was buying. Foremost in mind was that, if I let those meaningful designs melt, it would be a loss; I could have prevented the eradication of part of our Jewish culture.

Isaac, the man who had recently married me, was of course surprised by my sudden passionate uncommon enthusiasm in collecting Yemenite adornments. I was not interested in wearing any jewelry. Isaac wanted me to buy a necklace for the wedding but I was disinterested. I even didn't want a wedding gown, believing a light-gray business suit to be more practical than an elaborate gown useless after our intimate ceremony in the office of the Rabbi. Except for my mother, I didn't have anyone to invite for a celebration.

Isaac approved of all my decisions and judgments, even the unusual ones. My compulsive continuing acquisition of Yemeni artifacts in the 1950s expanded to the Bedouin, North African, and of course the ancient Roman glass and bronze designs. I was venturing back in time, not as a researcher or scientist. In the beginning my only wish was to prevent destruction. Slowly I realized the similarity, the repetitive patterns featuring the same symbols within ethnic groups. We all use the same meaningful forms, as we all are part of the same nature.

What had started as an impetuous decision was slowly expanding into a varied collection of a common link. Slowly I learned the stories connected with particular ornaments. Furthermore I was told that, through the centuries, working with precious metals was permitted to the Jewish minorities in the Middle East. This explained some typical Jewish ornaments appearing in Bedouin adornments like the star of David, the pomegranate and dove. Judaism and Islam both have restrictions on reproducing human features in the arts.

ALMOST A DECADE after my first impression of Israel, the Carmel Region during one summer in the late 1950s again became an active backdrop of pivotal circumstances. The location was near the Beth Lid military camp, where I first experienced my new home. On one of the round hills clearly visible from the road were the abandoned houses of a small Arab village whose inhabitants had fled during the 1948 War of Independence.

Prominent artists of Israel in the fifties started to rebuild the deteriorating settlement into a center for the visual arts; and as creative people began to congregate in Ein Hod, it became an artist colony. It was an opportune location close to the vibrant populated center of Israel, easy to reach from Tel Aviv and Haifa. There were prosperous Druze villages in the area, such as Usafia and Dalia, often visited by local tourists.

By that time I had become known by the established Israeli artists as part of the young generation. Thus I got an invitation to spend the summer months in a recently refurbished house. I took Mother, as well as my sons Benny and Raffi and our dog, Paca, for a summer in Ein Hod. Isaac stayed in Tel Aviv, preparing the coming season's repertory for the Cameri Theater.

My children's natural environment included growing up in a household filled with artists and creative people. The outdoors offered interesting encounters with nature that city life did not provide. In Ein Hod, the children met the fourteen-year-old village gardener Abdullah, a Druze who became their friend and a responsible guide to the surrounding area. He knew every trail around those hills, olive groves, and orchards. Abdullah was a constant guest for meals Mother prepared and he became our lifelong family friend.

For the first time I had the opportunity to work in a well-equipped studio for lithography. I made a brush drawing of two gliding birds on the scrubbed surface of the large stone I was given. Unconstrained drawing was my usual graphical technique, impulsively expressing my emotions.

The painted stone under pressure transmits the image onto paper. Then each print is individually numbered and signed. Every copy is slightly different as the pressure varies. Some of the prints are the so-called artist proofs; I didn't want to create many copies, as my preference was to draw my emotions, not accumulate prints. The artist is obliged to destroy the image on the stone after printing a numbered edition; thus no one can print additional images. Then the stone is cleaned with a hard basalt or granite scraper that brings the entire surface back to its pristine condition, in readiness for a new image. I applied the same intuitive way I paint, my firm line brush strokes, to the metal plates. Etching is similar to lithography but one works with acidic chemicals. I disliked that technique but appreciated the opportunity to participate in all that Ein Hod offered. I met new artists at this, my first leisurely creative time and opportunity, exchanging ideas about expressing feelings and thoughts.

There were some of the well-known artists like Marcel Janco, Rudi Leman, Moshe Mokady, Josel and Audrey Bergner, and others. We used to congregate at the village café, drawn by the spectacular sunsets visible from the terrace. Coffee with cardamom, hummus with pine nuts swimming in olive oil, fresh baked pita bread, goat cheese, and wine from nearby Rishon were the cherished evening treats. The café was run by a young bohemian couple who created a relaxed atmosphere most of us valued.

Nearing the end of my summer vacation, there was a fire in the nearby olive groves. This was a hazard of the dry season. We, the agile active souls of the community, exchanged our tools of art for shovels, building trenches around burning trees. The experienced men from the surrounding villages, while they appreciated our willingness to help, assigned us, the city slickers, tasks to ensure we would not hamper their efforts. Abdullah introduced me to his father and brothers, who arrived to keep the fire under control. The patriarch invited me to visit their home in Dalia before leaving for the city, which of course I promised.

Fires of war, those I was familiar with, were of a different kind. This was nature exhibiting its power in clearing the overgrowing shrubs, undergrowth, and infestations of vermin, Abdullah explained. He also made me aware that burned shriveled weeds would reveal the entrances to the many caves in the area. He asked whether I was interested in exploring them. Of course I was.

In the days after the fire before we went roaming looking around for caves, we searched for smoldering spots that could reignite. During those daily observation walks, I passed again and again a large olive tree that was charred to the ground. One of the tree branches probably had extended far out from the trunk as the fire had not reached it. The wood was left almost untouched by the devastation. The anthropomorphic-looking branch made me linger and return to the spot. The fire that had consumed the hill's vegetation inevitably brought for an instant some of my stashed away war memories into the forefront.

On our walks, Abdullah's knowledge and observance transformed him in my eyes from a considerate, decent teenager, to a young artist whose fast observations were profound. He understood that I was drawn to that particular tree. He carried that detached branch to the studio and advised me to start peeling the wood while it was still moist. He was a creative artist who recognized dramatic forms within nature. I immediately started to peel the wood into an over-six-foot abstract figure with an arm outstretched into the air.

In the remaining days after the fire, Abdullah and I explored the area around the partially scorched grove the fire had cleared from dense shrubs. He led me to one of the caves that his sharp vision had recognized and we agreed that if we found any coins they would be his; pottery or stone tools, mine. With all my experience, age, and what I believed sophistication, I had fun shoveling the earth searching for hidden treasure, like a child.

Abdullah, who had previously found some coins, was out of luck this time. After we had shoveled for several hours we unearthed two jars. One was a two-inch ceramic constructed without a wheel. It had one tiny handle and might have been a container to be carried around the neck, or maybe it was a medicinal or ritual object. The other jar had broken long ago, as a more recent break would have looked different. Years later I had my find examined by experts and it was identified as Bronze Age pottery.

Before I returned to Tel Aviv I urged some of the prominent art teachers in Ein Hod to open their studio doors to Abdullah and teach him how to develop his potential as an artist. I encouraged Abdullah to express his ideas and learn techniques and the craft. As promised, I spent a day in Dalia visiting his parents. I encountered the lavish traditional welcome and the appreciation of a friend. For years I could not eat a large amount of food and tried not to embarrass or insult my hosts but I had to taste the enormous variety of vegetarian dishes prepared for me. Abdullah, who knew my frugal eating habits, saved me from indulgent overeating by proposing to show me his village. Before we reached the edge of Dalia, he told me about his favorite cousin who lived there. He said Amal was a highly artistic seamstress creating embroideries I would appreciate. I imagined the woman would be like his mother, an overweight matron with a big smile, surrounded by racks of embroidered, mostly black, and rather shapeless dresses the women wore. The outline of dresses was supposed to conceal the female figure. Those beautiful embroidered ornaments in my opinion drew a second look, or were a teasing attraction, suppressed femininity possibly created.

Familiar with my own fears in hiding during the war, I understood the safety of hiding my gender in lawless times. The traditions here were supposedly sheltering and protecting women. Yet to myself, an adult female, stringent rules of behavior created by men exhibited a dark side. Overprotection was a diversion, curbing female creative expressions.

When Abdullah told me that his cousin was handicapped and lived by herself, I wanted to meet her. Her door was not locked. I was surprised seeing a young and beautiful girl sitting by the window, doing needlework. There was an austere feel in the room dominated by a large table with paper patterns and fabrics, and a couple of plain wooden chairs. There were no pillows or rags covering the floors like in Abdullah's parents' home. This was not a dwelling where guests frequented. It looked like a workshop of a lonely merchant.

Amal was apparently isolated from ordinary village relationships. She spoke like an educated person and probably read a lot, although I did not see any books in this room. She was extremely pleased to meet me, the pale young woman said. She wanted to hear about my work at the theater. I wondered if Amal ever saw a theater performance; she seemed to know quite a lot about the world outside the village. Her embroideries were as delicate as she.

Amal might have had polio when in 1950 the epidemic ravaged the entire region. She walked with great difficulty, leaning on her cane. Being handicapped made her an outcast. It reminded me of the Balkan villagers' superstitions. Here, people seemed to hold similar beliefs.

Two years later when I visited Ein Hod, I was again in Dalia and saw Amal. The only difference in her studio room was her beautiful crochet curtains featuring flying birds. I complimented her for her artistic and expressive capability. I liked this creative girl's courageous self-sufficiency.

MY WORK WAS in constant upswing. I was given the assignment to construct the interior architecture for Moadon Hateatron, the Theater Club in Tel Aviv. That project represented my most serious creative successes at that eventful period in my life. By that time, Abdullah had changed his name to Ovadia and planned to serve in the Israeli army as his older brother Joseph did.

I asked Ovadia to work as my assistant for the interior finishing in the club. My ideas were unusual because I wasn't trained as an architect. Ovadia was ready and capable to experiment with all my whimsical ideas that older craftsmen simply dismissed as wrong. From the unusual plasterwork on the walls, which I wanted to resemble a natural cave, the interior of the club was entirely unconventional, a radical departure from the club's usual designs. The end result was an unusual visual atmosphere with excellent acoustics.

My Yemenite and Bedouin jewelry collection became an exhibit, which added to the club's uncommon attractions. Insuring the exhibit was not in the budget, so Ovadia and I secured the adornments on colored patches of jute fastened with metal wire onto the chicken wire hanging on chains, fastened close to the ceiling in one of the rooms. At the bottom of those wire backgrounds we hung chains with camel bells. The weight of the bells and chains straightened the entire hanging and if anyone touched the displays, the bells would sound.

The jewelry was a beautiful and highly educational exhibit, linking the Roman glass adornments, shown in a display case, to the contemporary designs. The abundant history of this human highway through the centuries repeated the same basic symbols, articulated by diverse ethnicities, as an unbroken link. Our nature is the same. Through time only the materials changed. Our pivotal ideas are linked to our basic needs and fears: the symbols of fertility, power, and status, the craving for lucky charms and defenses against the "evil eye," longing for love, fear of death.

The exhibit featured several contemporary silversmiths who resided in Ein Hod as well. It gave those artisans exposure to a wide and varied audience for an entire year. During the day the exhibit included showings for schoolchildren.

THE THEATER CLUB was an altogether creative success. Isaac was the daring producer of a political satire program, its practical democratic purpose combined with sensitivity to civility and substance, all wrapped up in a place that generated well-being through entertainment of meaningful art. I became responsible for the entire visual ambiance and atmosphere and functionality of the place, including the stage with all the equipment, the acoustics, and the lighting, which refurnished a gray cellar into a combination of club, pub, and theater.

Fortunately I was ignorant about the proportion of the plan. My utter lack of experience for such a large project instead of intimidating me became a playful challenge due to my naive view of the task, not knowing what a club or pub was supposed to be.

In hindsight, my latent immaturity helped me be bold. Part of my frozen teenage mind in wartime turned into daring creativity. Isaac knew it and confidently encouraged my spontaneous playfulness. Lack of finances became an asset as I turned to discarded lanterns of fishing boats for illuminations and made collages of international old theater posters that were in forgotten storages. From the wineries, I found discarded small barrels to serve as tables and made additional tables from tree trunks.

The well-established architect Dov Carmi, who built the new Cameri Theater in Nachmany Street, liked my initial ideas and furniture models. I really did not need too much encouraging to plunge into the enthusiasm of creating.

It was altogether fortunate for the successes of the club that Frank Peleg, a formidable pianist and musician, became our musical director. The talented lyricist and political satire writer Dan Almagor started to write for our stage, and the actor-director Joseph Milo, with his imagination influenced by his wife Jemima's touch of French artistry, made the Theater Club in Tel Aviv a big success. Soon we were asked to expand and open a second club in Haifa, adjacent to the new municipal theater.

Almost daily I was on the train to Haifa working on the project. During the summer school holiday, my sons accompanied me, having breakfast on the train. My work was fun for my children.

After we opened the club in Haifa, two of Ovadia's brothers worked there for quite some time. After finishing the project in Haifa, my involvement in both clubs began to slow down. I was expecting my third child. My activities at the club subsided and I returned to painting, an activity I had postponed for years.

It was a surprise when one morning Ovadia's younger brother Hamud suddenly came to visit at my home in Tel Aviv. His distressed expression obviously showed there was something amiss. Hamud said that he came to say good-bye because we were friends. He had to leave Israel, go into exile, because it was a family honor affair. I knew not to ask him any question because I respected our different religious and behavioral codes. We hugged, I bid Hamud farewell, and he left with tears in his eyes.

A family honor affair, that silent active part of ancient tribal code, is usually shrouded in most societies. Yet they are not abandonned. The Druze religion is secret; Ovadia had told me that some time ago. Of course I didn't ask any questions. Isaac and I were sad about Hamud's departure, drawing his family into the tragedy of silence and social withdrawal.

I AM RECONSTRUCTING the events many decades later. They feel like centuries, possibly because so much has occurred in what became a multilayered, eventful embroidery of that period and onward. The colors have faded, but the structures of these events have remained. My memory, mainly being visual, works the same way as my vision. The result is unified in the brain from the fragmented slivers of reality.

While I underwent substantial changes through time, past experiences etched in memories remained snapshots with sharp focal points surrounded by the softer, less essential elements. What and whose images I chose to retain, I can retrieve. I feel rich with my abundant memories, even the painful ones that come to the surface, unexpected at times.

OVADIA HAS BEEN and remained a pleasant past and occasional present in my mind. Occasionally we met through the decades in Tel Aviv and New

York when we had exhibits. He really developed into a fine artist and I feel good to have recognized and encouraged him in his artistic inclination.

Recently I had the opportunity to see on the Internet some of Ovadia's paintings for an exhibit in Germany. One painting brought back for me a recollection. It is an eerie portrait of a pale young woman with sad eyes surrounded by a dark background. I remember the crocheted curtains with the flying birds I admired decades ago. I would have liked them in the painting, but they were absent.

roaming with ease waste depths

a silver sliver above the waves

I wish

to be like the flying fish

a butterfly of the sea

Round Square

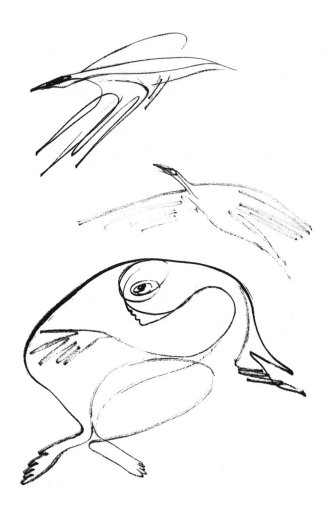

how long does it take to produce art

is the outcome in the time split of a lightning strike

as intensive energy collides and reverberates

with or against rhyme and reason

or

an idea sets out on an effortless glide

emulating an elegant raptor sifting the surrounding

in innate never sate scrutiny

on a lofty thermo flow of creative pride

perhaps

inventions grow throughout an entire life

slowly while a time hourglass fine sand seeps

grain by grain and word by word weaves the attire

exposing raw emotion nudity

Viewing the groomed vineyards of northern Italy, with their well-tended fertile fields intersecting populated areas, was my intended relaxation. The bus trip traversed several small towns I would otherwise have missed, due to lack of time. I at least wanted a glimpse of those. Moving at a slow pace felt right. This was the end of my vacation. Traveling by myself, this was my first carefree time after many years at the theater as a set and costume designer. My overly self-confident, almost daredevil project to build the interior of the Theater Club was what had earned me this almost two-month journey through France and Italy. I enjoyed the frugality of local train and bus rides, in contrast to the museums and opulent artistic wealth in the churches. I was discovering the abundance of human energy that fueled the creativity I was familiar with through my studies.

Stops were short. The villages looked rather similar, but I enjoyed the predictability of their design. Their pattern of sameness exuded tranquility. Repetitions create a familiarity, which becomes protective. Used to a chaotic past, I appreciated the soothing, low-key surroundings of the inevitable round square. A church stood on the perimeter of this central piazza, which featured a fountain, a saint, or both. Gently winding streets extended outward into the town.

People here had experienced the same war as me, only my injuries were extending into a pattern of historic repetition, inflicted through vicious destructions, which followed a frequently felt ceaseless antisemitic discrimination—recurring destructions leading to genocide of the Jewish people and culture. This existed in my bone marrow. The background of my family's history taught me to keep the past in my mind, but it goaded a vigilance in me for more information and further observation.

People here were veterans of battles. I noticed the scars in the deep furrows of tired, aging faces. But they also had pride. The cradle of the Renaissance was visible all around. Even in the desolation of war, the people shared cultural achievements, whether through art or exhibiting personal traditions, and this provided them comfort, a firm anchor of identity, a sense of belonging to the place they inhabited.

My journey in Italy started in Rome. After days and miles of inhaling the splendor, I took the train to Florence. Due to flooding of either the Tiber or the Arno, or both, our train stopped halfway, and we were in the open countryside for hours. I had not taken any food for the relatively short distance. To my good fortune, the third class was crowded with numerous local passengers, mostly men with baskets of local delicacies. They generously offered food and wine, which I gratefully enjoyed until we arrived in Florence. My Italian was extremely limited, but I spoke French. At that time, no one in Italy would acknowledge understanding German. When I said I also spoke Swiss-German, we communicated in three languages. I told them that I lived in Israel and came to Italy to see the art I had studied, and that I worked in the Tel Aviv theater. Our conversation became animated. Curiosity about Israel in the 1960s, my work, and my traveling alone created many questions. I showed photographs of my young sons and my husband, who was taking care of them in my absence. We became engrossed in opinions about the present postwar time. My fellow travelers turned the delayed arrival into cherished insight about the people who were part of Northern Italy. They allowed me, the traveling stranger, to feel accepted and included. In France, weeks earlier, even though I spoke the language, people seemed to me much more reserved and self-absorbed.

MEANDERING THROUGH ITALIAN settlements on the bus journey to the port of Genoa, on my way to catch the ship home to Israel, I was summing up impressions of my vacation. The bus driver did not announce names of places we passed, or maybe I was not paying attention. I was observing the local commuters. I liked the ride and the road.

Looking at the approaching small town, what appeared to me extraordinary were the sudden, unusual number of birds. They seemed to be all around. Flocks fluttering between tree tops, covering the roofs, flying in large formations as though migrating. The bus was meandering through what probably was the main street of that small town. There was a huge crowd on the central square. With so many people in the piazza, it may have been market day. I cast a fast glance at the square and realized the reason for the commotion. There was a sculptor mounting figures, apparently made of clay, onto a wooden podium. The spectacle must have drawn those many onlookers.

From a distance, on the bus, my first impression of the sculpture was of pale human figures, reminding me of Rodin's *Burghers of Calais*, the unforgettably monumental yet explicitly individual sculpted human figures in bronze I had recently admired in Paris. The several statues standing in the square were tragic human figures. I felt like a voyeur looking at a tragedy from which I wanted to recoil, perhaps the artist's very personal drama. The bent figures were standing inert, hopeless, powerless, lost, defeated, indicating doom.

The bus stop was close to that main square and a couple of new passengers joined us debating loudly, reminding me of Israel where people often talk to each other simultaneously. It resembles disagreements but it is just a way of voicing one's opinion. After one month in Italy I already identified some words from that communicating duet. The discussion continued in an animated way, therefore I started to pay attention, but it took me a while to understand that they were talking about the sculpture in the square. As they repeated the word *pane*, meaning "bread," it hit me. I had assumed that the figures had been made of a pale clay. But they were made out of bread.

EVEN AFTER MANY decades I recall the jarring effect as I realized the fact. That artist's choice of material for his statues still evokes feeling and thoughts. The sculptor had chosen to construct those figures from bread, a matter so intertwined with our life, the basic nutrient, harvested out of the soil, the earth, a symbol of our transformed cycle of existence. The artist kneaded the soft bread like it was clay and clad his constructed human form with intertwined symbolism, ingenious and original because of the sculpture's size.

Art has a stimulating effect on my brain, producing a quite accurate visual memory. Art filters into me and often becomes symbiotic in its energy to reconstruct emotions of past events.

Figures made from bread triggered my early childhood memories. As many children do, at mealtimes, I formed tiny figures from soft bread. I hid mine as I was not to play with food. And of course how could I ever forget the absence of bread, which later on, during the long years of war, I craved. I used to dream about eating fresh bread and woke up in the middle of night even more hungry than I had been the evening before, when exhausted I fell into perturbed rest.

WE LEFT THE village, the sculptures of bread, the square crowded with people anticipating the spectacle, and the enormous number of hungry birds providing the show the sculptor had planned. He was experiencing the demise of his creation. I was overwhelmed by my imagination. I thought the road would provide relief for me after the shock of knowing what I saw, but from which I could not disconnect. I continued to imagine what I was spared to witness. No green hills with castles or ruins of such could distract me from what I knew was taking place. The artist had intended that outcome for his sculptures. Why did he wrap them in bread, the invitation for birds to devour? I had seen the flocks congregating. My mind was there on that square. It was no relief that I was not witnessing the feeding frenzy, because I knew it was taking place. Was the sculptor there in the crowd of onlookers? Was he watching the destruction of his creation? Why had he condemned his own work to death?

Maybe the man had to relive experiences of his Second World War torments, fears, deprivations. Or was this his way of coming to terms with his hurt of irretrievable loss? Was this man repeating a self-punishment? Desperately looking to be absolved from what he couldn't pardon himself? Is it possible this was for the artist just one notch less than the ultimate self-punishment? The sculptor might have had the urge to live through the process of his death, the complete giving up of control.

Would I have stayed to watch the agony of my fellow artist, having his creation devoured? I don't know if I could have turned away and disconnected myself from looking at the birds feasting. Would I have become mesmerized by the spectacle of gore? What draws me to watch images of vultures stripping a carcass? Is it the fear of death that keeps me connected to the massive murder during my youth, which inspires me to view existence and death, within all its creative forms expressed in the arts?

Art, I believe, expresses what our brain creates into a feasible even ephemeral form, beyond the verbal or visual and musical explanation. The capability to remember, to re-experience an emotion after decades, is such a contribution to the affluence of the mind, it brings back the image of that event, including my imagined conclusion.

nameless artist I know you intimately

although we never met

we are the tireless messengers

before random strangers

because we both dare bare our core

you are the brother I neither had

nor ever will forget

Kaddish for Uncle Borosh

surfacing like humble bubbles

are minute memories

until a vital beam creates star sparkles

renewing luminosity

It was a large square red brick building I knew well, as it was the center of all the Jewish community activities as far as my childhood memories go. In the beginning of the 1930s, I started to wear the school uniform consisting of a black apron covering the front and back and tied on the sides. Our school bags were worn like backpacks.

My family indulged me and granted me wishes that, at times, were unusual. They encouraged me to pursue my whims, even unconventional ones, such as working with what would be considered unsuitable tools for a girl of my background and age. I loved to cut wood with a jigsaw and, on the cutouts with an electrically heated pen, burn the contour of my designs. The scent of accomplishment—of smoke, paint, turpentine, or polishing my product—gave me pleasure. I gave my gifts to family members for birthdays and holidays. My parents were probably happy when I started preschool, where my constant messy bustling was to be diverted. The school was on the Jewrejska Ulica, managed by the Jewish community center of Novi Sad. The entire complex consisted of brick buildings around our large synagogue, a lavish edifice with an elaborate portal and colored glass windows depicting biblical scenes. In between the buildings was our schoolyard. Only sparse sunshine fell on that playground, and its shadows brought a bleakness to our play.

My first grade teacher was called Borosh Baci by his pupils. In Hungarian, Baci may also be used for an elder, but for us it meant "uncle." He was tall with horn-rimmed glasses, a graying mustache, and military-style cropped hair. He had the pleasant attitude of a benevolent family member who was always patient with the slower children and had a twinkle in his eyes for the more inquisitive, rambunctious ones. We loved him because he would clarify what we could not understand. We were at the age of encountering the wonders of life. Uncle Borosh churned my curiosity to explore further. He led us through four years in most subjects, including Bible studies. He used to say that I was going to marry a rabbi since I had so many questions.

I remember people who touched my life at a geometrical tangent, not intersecting yet diverting my energy into a particular direction. I believe the genuine influence and conviction of those magnetic individuals shifted the way I changed my directions knowingly or not, toward ideals and ideas those educators personified. As an ardent Zionist, Uncle Borosh influenced my later decisions. So did my literature teacher in junior high, Ms. Glushatz, who always encouraged me to express my thoughts. Those educators are vivid in my memory. They reappear like bright comets dashing by, now and then, on my horizon, still illuminating and triggering my creativity.

Thinking about it now, the Second World War feels as if it lasted many lifetimes. That incredible nightmarish period had entirely blocked the sunlight and let darkness swallow the years. The horrific reality of one group selected for complete annihilation by another group raised questions that will remain painfully unanswered. Some of us children of that time randomly survived against all odds; but that destruction was imprinted with our individual experiences. That war era and its postwar decades created a novel vocabulary, expressing or suppressing what no one wanted to talk about or listen to.

When the Nazis withdrew from Belgrade, I tried to hold on to the minute dignity left in me, while facing yet another reality, how to build an existence with not much substance, with neither tools nor any financial means beyond what I earned to support Mother and myself.

The melancholy of the first postwar years completely changed at the beginning of 1948 when I traveled back to Novi Sad, where I was born. For the first time since the end of the war, the opportunity arose to make a difference in my life and for my mother. We could legally leave Yugoslavia and emigrate to Israel, although the state had not yet been declared. Fighting for the land where we could settle, we, the rejected, the homeless and unwanted Jews, eventually built our new home. The countries where we and our forebears were born and lived as productive members of communities, whether in Europe or in the Middle East, had either expelled us or at least encouraged us to leave.

Some Jewish organizations had by then arranged with the Yugoslav government to let the remaining small group of Jewish survivors emigrate. Once immigration to Palestine under the British Mandate became legal for us, I started the process in the Novi Sad municipal bureaucratic maze, which merged the old administration with the new law's confusing red tape.

Since childhood, careful plans had been made for my sister Susan and me—for our education and for our financial well-being. The beautiful house in Novi Sad we inhabited was secured in our names as part of our dowries. As a surviving co-owner, I inherited my sister's share. According to the existing laws I also inherited my grandmother's real estate in Novi Sad, a large corner house with fourteen tenants. Before the war the rent was part of her livelihood. My inherited real estate did not give me any income. I was liable for the repairs and taxes, and could not collect the rent as I lived, studied, and worked in Belgrade. Grandmother's house was for me a burden not an asset. The typical security symbols, like ownership in postwar Yugoslavia, were more liability than income. Therefore I acted intuitively. I relinquished all my real estate to the government I despised. Leaving the country meant the end of my budding career as well as the relationship with the man I was in love with for the last two years.

At fifteen I had left what represented my existing life ingredients, people I loved, my parents and home, to stay alive. At fifteen my life was physically threatened. At twenty-two, my freedom of expression was in danger. To free myself from dictatorship was so essential that everything else became less important. The combination of my childhood images, taken from books, stories, and my imagination, came together to form my perception of the Land of Israel. Those ideas must have matured, because when the opportunity arose, I promptly acted to get out of Yugoslavia, despite the ongoing fighting over the establishment of the State of Israel. I wanted to join those who were establishing the state where Jewish Holocaust survivors were finally going to be welcome. Even though the Nazis had been defeated, I had to get away from Yugoslavia, where Jews were barely tolerated. The hurdles before me emerged in numerous forms; for many months, I completed multiple documents, visited many offices, paid numerous fees, and traveled from Belgrade to Novi Sad in order to obtain permits. Bureaucracy was the price for freedom.

The crates with books to be sent to Israel were thoroughly checked by government officials before they were sealed. I had to remove the rare books my mother had salvaged from home during the war. I gave those prohibited editions to the few people I considered my friends and who appreciated rare books. I was leaving with no valuables and no regrets.

In Novi Sad in 1948, we gathered at the Jewish community center to begin our journey to what was still Mandatory Palestine. It was here that I met my old grammar school teacher Uncle Borosh. The center was once again a pivotal magnet. We survivors would linger, reconnecting and searching for bits of information about missing family members and friends. "Did you see . . . ?" "Did you meet . . . ?" To let go of hope was to give up the fight for life, give in to death.

Uncle Borosh had dramatically aged. I don't know how he had survived the war. Whatever his experiences had been were now showing on his face. I too was run down, weathered, definitely not the kid he knew, yet we immediately recognized each other. As shabby as we all looked, my old teacher was in a radiant mood, telling me he was waiting to get his permit and travel to Palestine with the first group. The Yugoslav freighter *Radnik* was about to sail from Rieka on the Adriatic to Haifa. Uncle Borosh sounded really happy. I told him that I was going to follow in the second transport. With a twinkle in his eyes, I remember he said that my decision did not surprise him, adding with a smile the sentence I had not heard for years but knew from childhood: "Next year in Jerusalem."

IT WAS THE summer of 1949 and I was already working in the Tel Aviv Cameri Theater as assistant set designer. Having gotten the job after being in Israel for only two weeks made me feel very fortunate. Every moment since my arrival had been saturated with rapidly changing and exciting events. I did not wait to be settled somewhere in the country. I knew I could find my line of work either in Jerusalem or Tel Aviv, the two prominent cities for theater activity. It was essential for me to act fast as I had only enough money to keep my mother and me afloat for about one week. I wanted to work as a set designer, and not wait as a passive newcomer to be offered something by the agencies that were overwhelmed with the sudden enormous immigration. The fast pace in Tel Aviv convinced me that Israel and the theater were the right place for me.

I arrived at the theater with my portfolio of set and costume drawings as they were preparing for the new season play "The Shadow," a political satire written as a fairy tale. Leopold Lindberg, a well-known film and theater director from the Schauspielhaus in Zurich was a guest artist for the production. He liked my drawings and wanted me on the team. The painter Moshe Mokady was the art director. I had one week to build a model of the set for the stage director Lindberg. Within three days I finished the model and had some of my additional ideas ready, including the technical drawings for building the set and specifications of wood and canvas and paint. I was hired immediately. I highly appreciated Mokady as a fine painter, but he was not a set designer. Working together was an enriching experience for both of us, developing into friendship. That production became a great success for the Cameri, and it introduced me to my career. This was my new home.

Everything developed with utter speed. Shortly after starting my work at the theater, I became engaged and married. My husband was a rabbi, as Uncle Borosh had predicted. Although Isaac was not a practicing rabbi, his background, education, and personality offered me an entirely novel relationship with a man who was extremely well balanced in relating to others. He had an honest respect for me as a woman, my need as an artist, and my core as a free individual. I had found my ideal partner. Beside the attraction, this was the first time I had absolute trust in a man. I wanted Isaac to father my children. It was an emotion I had never previously experienced.

Isaac had studied in Hebron and Bnai Brak but decided not to work as a practicing rabbi. The rise of Nazism in the 1930s led him to pursue education in the Polytechnic in Haifa. Later, Isaac became active in the Haganah movement. As artistic expressions and artists captivated him, Isaac turned to the existing Habima Theater youth group. That involvement led him to form a cooperative, the base that created the Cameri Theater.

Despite different backgrounds and our difference in age, Isaac let me experience an entirely original relationship with a man who understood even what I did not say. Isaac, my partner in life, was an enormous emotional support, a man who knew how to love generously.

BY THE EARLY 1950s some people from Novi Sad, from my childhood, now lived in the suburbs of Tel Aviv. Because they were not part of the Cameri's regular audience, my contact with them was infrequent. My life was evolving and revolving around my family and within the Israeli artistic and political social scenes. Nevertheless my activities in the arts were known in the Novi Sad circles. This occasionally resulted in get-togethers. Whenever we met, our talk inevitably gravitated toward our childhood in Novi Sad or our war experiences, reappearing as a refrain. In those rare yet predictable conversations, I asked if anyone knew where Uncle Borosh had established himself in Israel. The answer was a general outline of what had happened in Novi Sad prior to the first group leaving Yugoslavia.

After the first transport was approved to leave for Haifa, in 1948, Uncle Borosh had not been given permission to immigrate. The reason for the denial was that he was too old and since no one was around to take responsibility for him in case of emergency, he could not receive the travel permit from the Jewish agency.

I felt devastated at not having known about the denial and its reason. Worse was the horrific consequence of that rejection. Uncle Borosh committed suicide. He had hanged himself.

That fact hit me on many levels. First, I would gladly have signed a commitment for my teacher had I known he needed it. After all, I signed such a paper for Tessa Rakosh, a young woman I barely knew. Tessa was the sister of Lea Rakosh, whom I knew from grammar school, and who did not join our exodus. I helped Tessa, who was confined in a wheelchair as a polio victim since childhood. She needed someone to sign and accept responsibility, as well as someone willing to carry her and her wheelchair during our journey to Haifa.

Uncle Borosh, that lifelong Zionist and respected educator, was ignored by the Jewish survivor community of Novi Sad. I had been working in Belgrade, preparing to leave for Israel in the summer of 1949, not knowing what went on in Novi Sad several months earlier. There was nothing left for me but at some point to talk about it. That sobering fact about our behavior as survivors triggered a disquieting chain of thoughts. Had the inhumanity we experienced made us abandon our own humanity? Was our utter lack of sensitivity toward our fellow man the result of our emotions, including compassion, wasting away? Was our postwar detachment, resulting in indifference, the conclusion of a long period of prolonged personal fear, having lived with lethal danger? Had the Novi Sad survivors ignored Uncle Borosh merely out of self-involved negligence? Because that tragic event had been avoidable, it created for me a dark shadow, impossible to dismiss.

COINCIDING WITH THAT painfully disappointing information was my own work on a new production the Cameri Theater was preparing. It was one of Franz Kafka's stories, "The Castle," transcribed into a play by Max

Brod the publicist and friend of Kafka, who resided in Tel Aviv. Leopold Lindberg from the Schauspielhaus Theater in Zurich came as a guest director for that production, bringing his collaborator the set designer Theo Otto.

Theo, a non-Jewish German national who in 1933 opposed the Nazi Party, had been imprisoned. While incarcerated, he contracted tuberculosis and during his hospitalization succeeded to escape to Switzerland, where he survived the war. I met Theo when he came to Tel Aviv along with Leopold Lindberg.

The entire production, the collaboration with Theo, became a decisive moment in my professional life. Partaking in that complex production created understanding beyond the language we shared. Most of us in the theater were from central European countries. We grew up with a literature, music, and theater heritage based on centuries of frequently changed borders, but a consistently intertwined artistic harmony we shared and understood. In only a few weeks Theo taught me more than I had learned at the academy or through my work on sets in previous years. I had encountered a great artist, eager to share his knowledge.

For the first time in Tel Aviv, we used projected images on the theater stage. Gossamer net curtains were brought from Europe, one installed on the proscenium, the other mid-distance to the backstage. Lighting angles upon those mesh screens, Theo would transform them into an opaque state suitable for projecting images, or create the transparent exposure of a previously invisible new scenery, behind the second parting net curtain. The technique of the net curtains enabled a flow of action on stage instead of an intermission. Theo was a master of using minimal props and of lighting the stage during an uninterrupted performance.

He used to be a painter, Theo told me, and switched to set designing in Switzerland during the war to support his family. He became enmeshed in the dynamic lure of theater and could not leave the atmosphere. I was also finding myself drawn to the fascinating theater experience. Perhaps it is the attraction of our constant curiosity to be somewhere else, or someone else. The stage, costume, makeup, conjures that temporary magic.

After Theo saw my artwork, he advised me to concentrate my energy in what I was saying through my paintings. I was fortunate to encounter great teachers who had more confidence in me than I had in myself.

IT WAS IN the middle of Tel Aviv's hot summer when "The Castle" premiered. Entering the auditorium, the audience saw the stage as a dark gaping cavity, dense snow descending. The projection on the mesh curtain looked so real that it drew a loud gasp of surprise from the audience. For some, the sight could have been triggering memories of the freezing desolation of the 1942 and '43 wartime winters in Europe, or the familiarity with Kafka's writing that by itself could generate a chill.

Written at the beginning of the twentieth century, "The Castle" is a story of the ever-candid Kafka protagonist, the unpretentious, caring, spontaneous man, always entangled, struggling, losing his way in the maze generated by everyday life. The eerie presence of an enigmatic centralized authority hovers over everything, baffling the man's ineffectual routine. His stored papers are thrown around from their regular place by his malevolent helpers, creating disarray; or simple dialogues turn incoherent. The protagonist goes through his daily routine, which turns bewildering, as nothing is familiar anymore. As all is strangely surprising, culminating in disorientation, the man in vain tries to accomplish his work. Finally there are the basic temptations, the sexual attractions to which the main character succumbs. The main character in the drama is diverted by outer and inner forces. Kafka tells a prophetic vision of a time he did not fully encounter, yet sensed its imminent approach.

In spite of endless obstacles, Kafka's hero advances toward his goal to reach the elusive castle. He finally arrives in front of the fenced-in fortress, fog looming in the distance. Exhausted he lies down for a short respite but falls asleep in front of the locked gate while snow starts to cover him.

This was the performance of "The Castle" on the theater stage. I was part of the crew who made all the visual effects look and feel as real as possible for the audience. Images have the power to create in our brain a multifaceted, emotional kaleidoscope of feelings and transmit to our personal trove of similar images additional remote memories. Images are primal, and the impact is often strong and lasting beyond the spoken word.

In Kafka's stories most is left unsaid. Kafka invited us to inhale his rain-drenched gray sky of Prague, a city with central Europe's rich visual and artistic past that enhances imagination. How do Kafka's unspoken ideas fly in my mind? I have a somewhat timeless emotional intensity. When I let go of my secure frame of logic, the seemingly autonomous part of my brain triggers the connecting images from memory. It often results in a surprising continuity of how similarities in the human drama affect me. I do not understand the process. The need for a transmitted spark of a creative source becomes part of a craving; whether actively or passively, we depend on art, an emotional outlet we almost control.

For me, through all the performances, on that stage floor was Uncle Borosh, and snow flurries were burying him. When all meaning for his existence ceased, his life ran out of renewing luminosity.

I identify with the man

who carries overflowing images

engraved in his mind

scarred early in life I know

what war snapshots show

therefore I am compelled

not to forget atrocities

or look away from inhumanities

documented mounds of bare bodies

resembling parched branches

of chopped trees hurled onto piles for a pyre

rows of people with vital prospects

wantonly thrown into mass graves

in a murderous rage

by power perverts

on stage of the world

with sanity hibernating in deep sleep

a rare survivor may still be somewhere

and there is a brief time left

to share grief

The Calling Card

thus far I survived living

frequently smiling

my facial muscles increased resilience

to fit within the surrounding

where we all seek joy

even if shallow

I describe in stories or draw with lines that flow

to an eerie sphere of our absurd world

where abandoned ghosts tell their record

if there is a word for hurt

it is in a language

rarely heard

In the 1930s Novi Sad where I grew up, people of prominence kept crisp one-and-a-half or three-inch business cards in their vest pockets. These calling cards were engraved with names, professions, or social affiliations, and numerous titles, earned or bought. The post–First World War era had its winners and losers in the financial market. Nevertheless, in the Novi Sad Jewish community, everyone worked hard to maintain their elegance.

Vests were an important part of an elegant man's attire. Gold watch chains would stretch across portly waists. The vests were adorned with pockets where personal items were stashed. My father's pockets contained his silver card and cigarette case, an ivory cigarette holder, and an ivory toothpick. Father's gold watch and chain were of contemporary design, slim, and without ornamentation. The gold of men's timepieces symbolized affluence. Gentlemen who were fortunate to have made, inherited, or married into a fortune signaled their social status with the whimsical gesture of unbuttoning their coats. As a child I liked to watch how elaborate this ritual could become. With a slow deliberate movement of his thumb, a gentleman would unlock the cover of the watch, which would spring open to reveal its face. The actual time was of secondary importance.

Both my parents preferred the less flashy modern fashion. Mother did not have a card with her name. Instead she had a lovely gold watch with a face surrounded by an enamel and gold four-leaf clover. She wore her watch on a velvet ribbon in the color matching her outfit.

I was eagerly waiting to get my own wristwatch, but there were still a couple of years until my bat mitzvah at age thirteen. There was a ceremony in our synagogue where all the boys and girls coming of age within the year would participate on both sides of the bimah in front of the open sanctuary displaying the Torah scrolls. The girls were all dressed in identical pale pink long gowns with a garland of pink rosebuds on their heads and a small bouquet of roses in their hands. The boys wore dark-blue suits and prayer shawls. All were blessed by the rabbi after they recited the prayer of the day, in unison. It was an innovative way for the Novi Sad Orthodox synagogue to welcome to the ceremony both boys and girls.

I watched my sister, Susan, who enjoyed the first year of the new celebrants' lavish festivity, and I hoped that whoever was going to direct the ceremony would change the color of the dresses. Pale pink was good for my sister's darker complexion; I looked terribly pale wearing that color. As my bat mitzvah age approached, powerful forces began to carve up and swallow European countries, and celebrations were canceled in the Novi Sad Jewish community as the war began. The times became bleak with the rise of the Nazi threat. What I wanted for my thirteenth birthday was a modern large square steel wristwatch on a wide leather band. But I never wore the one I received. It was round and small. I felt insulted and ignored, having voiced the style I expected.

After four years in grammar school at the Jewish community center, I continued in the only middle school for girls in Novi Sad, the stepping-stone for higher education and social status. Since writing was encouraged, I started to compose poems and essays. I chose to share a desk with a very quiet girl, Nada, because no one wanted to sit next to her. We knew that she came from a poor working class family and was admitted to the prestigious school because she had passed the rather demanding entry test. That was good enough for me.

During the school year Nada told me she had tuberculosis of the lungs and she believed that was the reason the other girls avoided being close to her. I knew tuberculosis was a widespread affliction in Yugoslavia, but sharing a desk with her would not endanger me. There was one young man in our Jewish community who had tuberculosis and he was healed after some years in Davos, Switzerland. It was a curable disease, I perceived, and I was not afraid. We had an infirmary at school where we were regularly tested.

After the second school year began, I decided to continue to share the desk with Nada who was still not very talkative. She had gained some weight since the previous year when she looked rather scrawny. Because I was convinced her health had improved, it took me by surprise when she said that I would have the entire desk, as she was not continuing her studies. The school had expelled her. Nada had received good grades. It did not make sense.

Then she confided in me. Her father had been sexually abusing her for some time and now she was pregnant. The medical examination at the beginning of the school year had revealed her condition. As we parted, she seemed bewildered by the fact that she could not continue school and very frightened.

I was terrified of what was going to happen to Nada. We were twelve years old and never before in my life had I been so angry. In Serbian, Nada meant hope. It was taken from her. Even now, after so many decades and throughout my life, at times saturated with loss, pain, sadness, and disappointments, I am still angry.

There was complete silence about her expulsion until I wrote about the event. In class, we were free to choose our subject and I poured out all my feelings of the injustice perpetuated against Nada, who had been punished in addition to having been abused. With the war on my horizon, I already had my own fears about atrocities. Jewish refugees with stories from central Europe were arriving.

My teacher, Ms. Glushatz, loved the essay. However, my father was called for a talk in the principal's office. The subject was considered out of bounds for someone my age. Father told the principal he was proud I had spoken out. Without such strong support from my family, I probably would not have dared to voice my outrage, as I often did. Yet my essay did not create the huge uproar I had hoped for.

IN 1938, I encountered people who had fled the Nazis in Germany and antisemitism in Poland and had arrived in Novi Sad. The refugees lived with constant fears. It showed on their faces, in their voices, recounting their experiences. I learned about the Nazi brutalities in German institutions for the handicapped. I was not yet mature enough to be inhibited about asking the refugees personal questions. I only understood most of their answers in later years.

Two very nice young men arrived from Germany to find work as instructors at our community center. One became the Maccabi gymnastics teacher for the Jewish community sports club. Serge, as we all called him, was a great gymnast and coach who taught me a routine of daily exercises that was of real value during my years of strenuous farm work in hiding during the war that soon followed. The other refugee became our extremely good-looking assistant rabbi. All the older girls, including my big sister Susan, had a crush on the attractive teacher, so his Sunday school became the most popular, fully attended event in our community. There was constant guessing about whom Rabbi Mordechai Silver would marry.

When he traveled to Poland to be married, we assumed his bride would be as beautiful as a movie star. Instead our rabbi returned with a very plain-looking young woman. We small girls were disappointed. My sister said the older teenagers from Sunday school were insulted, and with scorn began circulating what they thought was a joke about the newlyweds. Since Rabbi Mordechai couldn't find a Jewish bride who was unattractive enough in the vicinity of Novi Sad, he traveled all the way to Poland to discover "the plainest girl of them all."

I didn't think the joke was funny. But nevertheless I asked the rabbi why he had traveled to find a bride. His answer not only convinced me that he had heard the joke, his serious face and words made me uncomfortable that I had asked. I told Susan the rabbi's answer. He said that he went to Poland to bring one Jewish girl to a safer home in Yugoslavia. There were no more jokes. It took me a couple of years before I understood what Rabbi Mordechai Silver really meant. By that time our home was as lethal as Nazi Europe could be. There was no safe place for the Jews.

Not even the finest Swiss gold watches plundered by the Nazi invaders could measure how our war years distorted time, existence, humanity, culture. Like a cosmic event, as if our planet were hit by a meteor, in the historic time blink of only eleven years, the Nazi rise and destructive rule equaled near extinction for us Jews. Nature's cyclic extinctions of species on our planet is bound to a different dynamic, never based on hatred or distorted ideology. Therefore nature's resilience allowed us, the few survivors, to sprout from a scorched base. Irreversibly marked by what became imprinted in us, we continued.

IN HIDING DURING the war, I acted as though mute. Then in the Communist era of selective freedom of expression, I curbed my voice in almost silence. It took me years to regain my voice.

NOW I HAVE a square wristwatch on a wide leather band. I have a card printed with my name on paper. I exist. The drawing introduces me. This linear image is like a biography to those who can read visual art. It took one brief instant to decide which of my many drawings represented me.

I WAS IN my comfortable midlife, with graying hair, slightly sagging skin, happy as a mother of three grown children, fulfilled as a woman, accomplished as a creative person. I had returned home from touring Europe, where several collectors again bought my work. I had successfully established the possibility of exhibiting in the United States.

I was barely back in Tel Aviv when Isaac, my husband of almost thirty years, had a heart attack. I took him to the hospital. He was recovering. For two weeks I spent the days at his bedside. Our adult sons were independent; only Shira, our daughter, was still in high school. I would return home to be with her in the evening. She was very close to her father and knew how my presence was important for his well-being.

Isaac was to be released from the hospital when he died in his sleep after having another fatal heart attack. Our oldest son, Ben, received the phone call in the morning and picked me up on the way to the hospital. When we arrived, Isaac had already been transferred to the morgue.

I knew death. Children of my generation in Europe were brought up to accept death; we were taught loss. I grew up with Jewish rites to part with the deceased by sitting shiva, in mourning for a week. Slowly we come to terms with parting; we absorb pain and loss. I had to see Isaac, to look at death, to part with him and feel the finality, a separation that had no continuity.

I was adamant about seeing the man I loved, not having him disappear like my loved ones who had vanished during the war. Now, again I felt powerless. Strangers were making decisions as if I didn't exist.

My initial state of deeply injured feeling turned to defiance. I didn't want the soothing talk of the nurse offering me a tranquilizer to make me docile and silent. I refused the doctor's apology, who said that the Chevra Kaddisha, the burial society, was in a hurry when they took Isaac away as it was a Friday burial, before the start of the Sabbath. I told the doctor that under the circumstances I wanted an autopsy.

Ben and I went to the burial society building adjacent to the hospital. Raffi, my younger son, joined us there. We were going together to tell Shira, who was in school that morning.

The man at the entrance of the Chevra Kaddisha refused to let me see

Isaac's body. My pain turned to anger. I had lost the man I loved and lived with, the father of my children. He had died a couple of hours ago. And here was someone preventing me from seeing my life partner. I was not giving anyone the right to order me around. I was determined not to have Isaac simply removed.

This was 1978, not the Second World War, and now I had questions. This time I was going to get some answers. Isaac had died and no one in the State of Israel could deprive me of my right to see my dead husband. He was supposed to be released from the hospital. I wanted to know why an unexpected second heart attack occurred. I said this in a voice no one seemed prepared for. I said it in the hospital and in the Chevra Kaddisha.

The man at the morgue tried to convince me that he could not leave his post at the entrance, and that there was no one else to accompany me to the basement where the bodies were prepared for that day's burials.

I offered my sons as guards at the entrance. They had both served in the army and knew what security meant, I said to the man, and if he was not going to accompany me to the basement, I would go by myself and recognize my dead husband. Reluctantly that shivering young man took me to the lower floor.

There was Isaac on one of the slabs, a slight familiar smile in his already frozen expression. It was a consolation to see on his face that he had not been in pain. I felt a chill as I put my hand on his forehead. It was cold. Life had left Isaac many hours before, but it left me my emotions for him.

I began to feel my loss of Isaac. My existence changed once again. I had lost that intimate, secure, shielding envelope of the man who knew me better than anyone else ever had.

I had learned to heal superficially, leaving uneven scars that can never regrow into smooth undamaged skin. My skin was frequently slashed but I never developed immunity against pain. In fact it may have even left me more vulnerable.

With Isaac's death my life flow was diverted. There was no place to run and hide. I craved a soft dark sanctuary, somewhere to be invisible. Isaac's was a natural death, not expected, but I had learned to accept the end of life. Although experienced at living with loss, I was again emotionally immobilized, reminded of my youth, without a respite to let reality slowly sink in. I had to continue with no allowances for time to heal. I had to find immediate and new solutions in my suddenly severe economic situation.

Shira was experiencing the enormous loss of her father for which I had no explanation or substitute. She worshiped her father, who adored her, and now he was gone. The only ameliorating reality was her deep concern about me. She had been mature beyond her age, but her loss put my teenage daughter onto a level identifying with me absorbing loss. We were both equally occupied with worrying about each other. We each put our own personal feelings on hold.

My sons were already establishing their families, but all of us felt the need to support one another. I at least had the experience of knowing how to withdraw into my own hibernation. Maybe it was helpful that I had to deal with numerous daily problems, forcing me out of my drift into a semi-lethargic state. I was clinging to all my former mental anchors to keep me afloat. I turned to the advice my father left me with when we parted for the last time: "Do not feel sorry for yourself. Whatever happens, do what you can, don't feel sorry for yourself." I had never forgotten or forsaken this legacy.

Isaac had given me our three children and a treasure trove of memories. Memories of our meeting each other and the precious time, love, and fun we shared. Some memories from time gone are trinkets cluttering my emotional space and some became the heirlooms I never want to lose, as they are the heritage I eagerly transmit to my descendants.

I have a huge storage of images in my memory and those I drew and painted, recording the decades. Most old drawings of people from my past are in disarray, as they represented my observation of human interactions I noted more than understood. Even personal emotional clarity is fading through the distance of time as failing eyesight sees them. Due to this distance the once sharp-edged outlines of events now have a softer contour. The reign of time on me is like the rain on pebbles. I feel smooth.

THROUGH THE YEARS my work was exhibited in prominent galleries in Israel and gained a following. There were people who felt connected to my work: musicians, other artists, writers with personal creative expressions of their own. Some people were emotionally drawn to the themes within my artworks. We all continue to seek and connect to art's magnetic energy. Artistic expression moves the inner compass in all of us. I believe creating or absorbing art opens a road to the different unknown—and therefore feared—"other," often hidden within ourselves.

Art stabilizes me in that constantly moving reality when I am losing my balance, when I become aware of the tilting ground and the speed of life whirling through time. Creativity reverses me from the whirlpool of complete powerlessness.

AFTER ISAAC'S DEATH, I plunged into intensive painting, preparing for an exhibit in the Amalia Arbel gallery in Tel Aviv. The gallery was known for the intellectual patrons who used to favor it. The gallery handled the press, which attended the opening in hope of news stories. For my show, the mayor of Tel Aviv, Shlomo Lahat, made an elaborate opening speech. Journalists who usually didn't write about galleries and painters gave me a generous write-up. Most reporters knew me from the Theater Club days, when all the famous foreign artists who performed in Israel would come after their concerts and gave many encores, as most of our audience was made up of fellow artists or people drawn to the arts.

IN THE SPRING of 1978, after Isaac's death, I needed more than favorable newspaper articles about my present painting and my set and costume designing days. The abrupt change in my life felt like being in a foreign country where I didn't understand the language. That was when the circle of friends I had acquired through the years became my comfort space.

What followed were shows of my work in my friends' houses. Private shows, lectures, and concerts had become a trendy activity. The first of my private shows was in the home of Noa Blass, a musician, a composer, an author, and an innovative educator in developing the musical discipline in preschool education. The many-faceted Noa was the driving energy of my group of friends. Soon after, Ruth Friedman, an economist in city planning, suggested I should have a show in her family home also; I happily agreed.

THE FINANCIAL ARRANGEMENT for showing my work in their homes was simple, friendly, and comfortable for all of us. My hosts preferred to acquire my works instead of taking a commission from the sales. The agreement generated what I needed: camaraderie with people I felt close to and an income.

My work rested on images that were dark, painful, desolate. The basic theme was how the Holocaust had influenced my views. I could never erase that irreversible reality. Through my work I was expressing images of how isolation, hunger, and fear form the artistic handwriting of a painter. I only dared to depict the unimaginable concentration camps in my abstract thoughts, as my war experience was that of a hunted creature, hiding for my bare existence, always ready to run and not be caught.

My paintings were not emotionally uplifting and therefore it was difficult to imagine them displayed in anyone's living room or across from a dining table. Usually it was intellectual and artistic viewers who appreciated and bought my work. Although private home showings were not advertised in the newspapers, my reputation as an artist had reached wider circles, including the theaters.

My host Ruth Friedman informed me that she was pleased about the interest the show was generating. Theater people were calling her about the new dates and times for the exhibit. Suddenly there was a buzz.

I had been a professional artist for many years. The increased interest should have made me feel self-assured, but I felt ambivalent. It brought to my mind the week of mourning, the shiva, for Isaac. Yehiel, Isaac's younger brother, was Mr. Begin's so-called right hand and was with us for the week of shiva. Numerous people from the theaters, including mediocre actors Isaac had helped stay on the payroll, did not even show up for his funeral. The few actors who visited my home were waiting in my living room to be present for the arrival of Prime Minister Menachem Begin. My apartment was crowded with government dignitaries, also waiting for their opportunity to speak with Begin. We create these multifaceted rituals of death.

As expected, Mr. Begin arrived in his private non-official capacity. We knew he was a private person of no pomp and a lot of circumstance. He did not visit as the elected political figure. People who were waiting to bring up their political agendas must have been disappointed. For Menachem Begin this was not a day in his office; he came to be with Yehiel. One of the officials from the Ultra Orthodox Party nevertheless tried to engage him in a conversation, mentioning how the deceased Isaac was a powerful painter, judging by the many canvases on the walls. We who knew Mr. Begin as a private person recognized the hardly visible smile as he said: "The paintings are the artworks of Isaac's widow." Yehiel, my children and, yes, even I smiled. Isaac would have laughed.

IN THE TIME almost immediately following, the actors did not maintain any contact with me despite my almost thirty years of marriage. Their sudden interest in my exhibit did not make sense. They had never shown interest in my paintings before, which led me to believe that they just wanted to see a forty-something distressed widow who, from an established social and artistic position, was now bereft and in financial difficulty. A show to see and be seen—not to be missed.

They did not dislike me; there was no reason for them to do so. For years they performed in costumes and on sets I had designed. I always adapted colors and styles of gowns that would make them feel comfortable performing. I knew each actor's idiosyncrasies and as a designer I thought it essential to help them in their artistic representations.

From the actor's perspective, I had come out of the unknown, with experiences they knew nothing about and were not interested in. They had either left Europe before the war or were born in Israel. Isaac was the eligible bachelor of that artistic milieu. And here I was, a stranger of twenty-three, an old maid by their standards, a recent arrival to the newborn State of Israel, suddenly assuming a prominent position in their circles, acknowledged in newspapers as an artist. I kept myself isolated from the petty theater intrigue and gossip; it bored me.

For almost thirty years I had known and worked with people and had successfully ignored their jealousies and betrayals. I had no friends in the theater. Their disregard of Isaac's funeral did not really surprise me. He was dead and of no use to them. Now, as so many showed interest in my show, I concluded it was mostly for the free wine and entertainment.

The new show stimulated my anticipation to meet the theater crowd in a different environment. It was a needed change from my disinterest in people since Isaac's death.

The painter in me quickly saw behind people's expressions. Most of the theater actors who came to the exhibit did not look at my work. The Saturday noon opening of the exhibit created a comic show for me. Like a choreographed dance between and around obstacles, when each move or step expresses the uncertainty of how to proceed, those people were shuffling from one place to another, avoiding the space where I stood. I caught furtive looks intertwined with those gazing at me. It began to be entertaining and I certainly needed amusement.

In situations that required a basic uplift, I could count on my emotional emergency rations drawn from my childhood memory sanctuaries, when my sister Susan would create games for us during the many somber occasions in which we had to participate. There were the long visits to our boring relatives where we had to be polite. We had to sit and listen to their numerous complaints we knew so well since they were repeated so often. Those litanies never interested us.

Funerals were less boring. We liked it when the grown-ups were unsure how to act. This was often amusing and even held surprises for us children. On most occasions Susan would find a solution to our boredom by inventing new games. Five years her junior, I always agreed to whatever she suggested, happy that she would let me participate in her game. At the cemetery she would ask me to count how many people genuinely cried, while she would count those who faked grief. During funerals or visiting the mourners at the shiva, she and I would retreat to a spot where we could observe everyone, unseen. Besides, in hiding, we could eat the numerous omnipresent sweets.

Our game had goals. We knew the people and their relationships and we could guess which mourners were really sad. With our shameless childlike instincts, we would figure out the adults' behavior. Especially the ones who showed grief by waving their large black-rimmed handkerchiefs like flags before covering their faces. Susan of course always earned the most points, observing and explaining the fake behavior to me. I, the loser in the guessing game, did not mind. I did not understand it yet, but always enjoyed a game when there was not much else to feel good about.

Standing in my exhibit at my friend's home, now a recent widow, for an instant I was once again feeling my sister's knowing winks at me. For a split second I felt her close. I was back in the place where I grew up. It was good to sense Susan right there in my mind. After many decades since she had been killed in the war, the thought of her provided comfort.

Tel Aviv of the 1970s was as provincial as prewar Novi Sad. Now this was my home. Maybe it was I who did not fit in here.

There were so many ghosts accompanying me. Could I, with my crowded past, squeeze into any home anywhere? I did not want to lose my ghosts. I diligently kept them alive in my paintings.

Reinvigorated through my spark of memory, I was ready to face life, the present reality, any people, whoever they were. I needed the money and had to sell my work. That was the purpose of the exhibit.

My host Ruth and I had already decided on our lower price list, because in spite of numerous viewers, there were no sales. As the day progressed, one of the drawings drew some attention and caused a dispute between a married couple. I knew them both. The woman was a prominent radio anchor and I was pleased that she showed interest in my work. She obviously wanted that drawing as she moved back to it before taking the checkbook from her bag. That immediately provoked her husband to intervene, vehemently. I also knew the husband from years in the theater. He was one of the essential supporting actors.

I was a widow in financial difficulties due to taxes that were very high. My name was not on the deed for the apartment Isaac and I owned for years and for which I helped to pay the mortgage. Our lawyer had omitted my name from all the deeds, home and business properties. I never checked. It turned out to be a very costly negligence on my part. After almost thirty years I had to pay taxes as if I were a stranger who had just inherited these properties. Otherwise I would lose them. Now I was vulnerable on many levels. A widow was not protected in a couple-oriented society with archaic laws.

With an array of distracting thoughts, I was forcing myself to focus my full attention on the reality of my exhibit. The actor was explaining to his wife that they should offer half the price listed for the drawing she wanted. I would agree to it since I had to. It was no secret that I was left with debts and no forecast for a fast recovery. Of course I could not miss overhearing that actor who, after all, had been on stage for years and was trained to make his words carry. Maybe he did it intentionally so I would hear what he was saying.

The actor was correct about my finances. I had known what it meant to be without money since I was fifteen. Strangely I never felt poor. It seemed interesting that people who knew me and my decades of work would consider me easily intimidated.

I regarded myself as a person who had good luck in my life, and painful losses to the same degree. What I always accepted was life in its versatile nature and my adjusting to the predictable and to the unforeseen.

The actor was superficial in his understanding. Maybe that was the reason he wasn't awarded leading roles on stage. I would give my work as a gift, but I was never going to sell to anyone who was haggling for the price of my art, like one buying discounts after the holidays.

My friend Ruth, who organized the show, embarrassed by such an unexpected and devious attitude from the actor, nevertheless reluctantly asked me if I would agree to sell for half the price. We both knew the importance of having a red dot on a painting in an exhibit. It would invariably boost sales. Of course she was right, but I said no; I would buy my own drawing for the full price.

I asked Ruth to put the red sticker on the frame, without divulging the buyer. The drawing was sold.

That drawing is printed on the calling card that I have used to introduce myself ever since.

if I reside on an anthill I must be an ant

yet I sing like the cricket in the fable

who dares

in spite of advice and the foreboding scare

of freeze and famine's empty table

I'll voice my minute part

maybe lacking the correct key

sing my tune in a wrong beat

and miss a perfect pitch

but let my feelings ring

unraveling the thread

until the end of the string

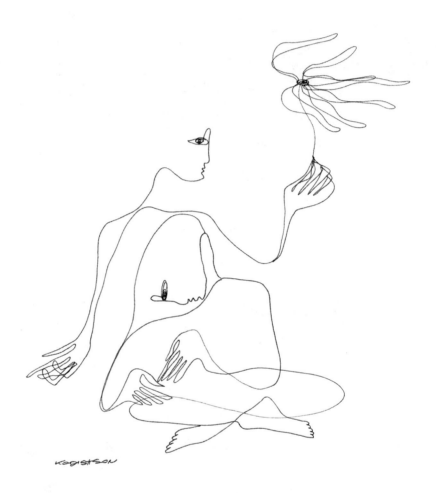

The Olive Tree

a tree will reveal in each ring individual deprivation

a story of parching drought

or ceaseless rain as the ground was swept away

and roots stripped of procreation

leaving desolation to reign

damaged trees tell recorded memories

we are required to disregard

if hit hard

urged to go on or impelled to forget

engraved injury

as grief is received

in brief curiosity

Encouraged to explore from an early age, I was curious, ready for unfamiliar, even strange culinary experiences, jolting spices, or at times bitter-tasting food. What was important to me was the color and aroma of the new edibles. I loved to eat any food in any shade of green. Fruit was my favorite, even the unripe, slightly tart peaches, crunchy with the scent of fresh greens. Of course I also loved sweet cherries, especially the large dark-red ones.

During my preschool days, I would regularly accompany my grandmother to the market. Treating me as her equal, she would not talk down to me as grown-ups usually spoke to children. I liked that, even though I often didn't understand what she said despite my careful listening. She must have repeated particular phrases, because I remember them. "People spend a long time and carefully build up lies, and then they forget what they previously said. It is simpler to tell the truth as it is easier to remember." And, "Some people will whine all the time, even though no one is really listening. Complaints do not change anything."

I liked her resourcefulness and blunt explaining. If a subject were unpleasant, she'd say it with candor. Grandmother would provide stories for my curiosity. She would take me to the workshops of the craftsmen who did repairs in her apartment building, after she collected the rents and complaints. She owned a house with fourteen tenants, a corner building in a working-class neighborhood with tiny vegetable gardens in the inside courtyard. The building was situated in a mostly Serbian-populated part of Novi Sad. Close by was a baker who had the best-tasting rye bread in town. Whatever the weather Mother insisted that once a week we take that lengthy excursion to Sava Vukoviceva Street. She believed in brisk walking, and excursions to fetch the well-baked dark bread were part of our routine. With Grandmother excursions were not routine. I loved to go with her as each outing was different, especially the shopping activities. On market days, live chickens would be carried in our maid Paula's basket. We would stop at the synagogue compound where, behind our Jewish grammar school and the synagogue, was a small building for the kosher slaughtering of poultry. Paula would carry the basket to the slaughterer, following Grandma's instructions, to have "it" done according to the Jewish ritual. As curious as I was in everything around me, I never wanted to witness what happened to the chickens and geese, even if killing the animals was done in what Grandmother said was the right way.

Paula would take the loaded baskets home and prepare our meals. Mother was baking pastries and cakes, as that was what she really loved to do. On our way back home, Grandmother and I would at times stop at the Pilisher Deli on the Jevreiska Ulica, the Jewish street in Novi Sad. That was what I always silently hoped for, as food from that deli tasted different from what was prepared at home. The smell in the store was appetizing, and I remember the display of splendid-looking delicacies. That was a place where Grandmother would compromise her otherwise strict dietary rules. Grandmother would buy fine foreign cheeses and all kinds of marinated fish and pâtés. What I wanted in that deli was in a large glass jar on top of the counter. That container was filled with what appeared to be enormous cherries. I had never seen anything like that anywhere else. As if they were polished, they were shiny with a somewhat darker color than the cherries I was familiar with. With their promise of a different taste, they became all too desirable. I really wanted to eat them, yet they were not purchased. Grandmother was decisive about not buying the fruit out of that jar. My wistful staring at that glass container must have prompted the woman behind the counter to reach into the jar and present me with one dark fruit. She wrapped it in a paper napkin, telling me I could spit it into the wrapping if I didn't like it. I remember the jolt of my first taste of what turned out to be a large black olive.

I was prepared for a sweet cherry and what I got was a salty, pungent, slightly bitter taste—an oily, pine-smelling mouthful. But I swallowed my disappointment. This brief experience taught me not to show surprise when what I expected turned out to be the opposite. Later on, that suppression became a valuable lifelong advantage in controlling my reactions. I had wanted to be included in the world of adults and their tastes of life. But all too soon my wish turned into reality. A few years later, the Second World War reached us. Even the smallest children were included in the murder by the Nazis who occupied Serbia, where they killed the entire Jewish community mostly concentrated in and around Belgrade.

Registration of all Jewish families took place immediately after the disintegration of Yugoslavia in the spring of 1941. Disobeying the registration order meant execution. Some of us took that risk. Even survived. All those who obeyed the Nazi order were rounded up and soon taken across the river Danube to Zemun, the prewar location for agricultural fairs and entertainment. Already in hiding, I realized the irony in the sneering, arrogant choice of that place—a place associated with merry-go-rounds, carousels, and stands with gaudy merchandise, bringing to mind the smoke-filled air from the open fire with its roasted sausages called *ćevapčići*, the *ražnići* on skewers with chopped onion, all kinds of sweets, cotton candy, clowns, and puppet shows, and farmers showing and selling their prized animals and products.

The Staro Sajmište across the river was visible from the Kalemegdan Hill. A nature promenade overlooking the big waterways where the Danube from the north and the river Sava flowing from the west merge into an opulent body of water rolling east; this became the Nazi murder site with no survivors.

Knowledge of that horror soon followed the disappearances of many young Serbs and seeped toward those of us who were hiding in the vicinity. Meticulous hunts also followed those who from the start had fought the German occupation from strongholds in the mountains. Those events starting in 1941 are my permanent memories.

IN 1939, PRIOR to the Nazi onslaught on the Balkans, our family had moved from Novi Sad, our hometown, to Belgrade. My father believed that being in the capital city, where we were not known as Jews, gave us a better chance to survive. When the German occupation of Serbia began, we decided to separate and hide. All my fanciful childish and early teenage daydreams and self-deceptions disappeared immediately from my altered reality when I irrevocably left my family. I said goodbye to everyone who to me represented love, security, protection. I took what I could carry in my backpack and went to hide with complete strangers.

RECONSTRUCTING EVENTS FROM my memories can conjure enigmatic images. Details that for decades were concealed within the crevasses of my brain, I deemed marginal, unimportant, until they began to emerge into a pattern. Over the years I discovered those elements fitting into a coherent image of many seemingly unrelated events. As a child, I liked to look through the end of our binoculars that would distance what I viewed. The image became wide; I could see more and everything looked small due to the distance, but clear. Maybe memory is recorded in a similar way. Events far from the present, in hindsight, flow like rivulets connecting into a wider streaming past.

SOME YEARS PRIOR to the beginning of the Second World War, in the early 1930s, my grandmother's youngest brother, Lazar, visited what we knew then as the Holy Land. Upon his return, he brought mementoes for us to choose from. At that time I was in elementary school. What took my fancy was a plaque of olive wood with a carved bas-relief of a strange round building and a pointed roof. I was told that this was a sight in Hebron, the tomb of Absalom. I had no idea who he was. What I liked was the color pattern in the beautiful grain and the pungent scent of the wood. I remember the grown-ups' reaction when I chose my gift. There was surprise, a puzzled disbelief that I had chosen a tomb. I did not know it either then nor later on why that piece of wood, among many other trinkets more enticing for a child, was important to me.

Shortly before the Nazi roundup of our Jewish community in 1941, and before I left my home to go into hiding, I remember being upset that I couldn't take that olive wood plaque in my backpack along with the more obvious essentials. It must have been easier to be sad and angry about a trivial memento from my favorite great-uncle than the loss of my entire accustomed reality. After all, to go into hiding meant that there were so many other personal items I had to abandon. When I left home I had to suppress fear, sorrow, and the needed physical closeness to the people I loved. I had to suppress my tears. In silence I had to figure out how to deal with emotions crowding within me at once. The rebellious teenager's voice in me was muted in the din of exploding bombs during the unceasing darkness of the days, and the glaring fires that caused the nights' unbearable illumination, keeping me awake and in fear of being surrounded and incapable of escaping the flames. My present was irrevocably changed and so was my future; that is, if I were to have one.

As the German Army was marching into Belgrade on my fifteenth birthday, April 12, 1941, without delay, we had to burn all the identifiable Jewish symbols we had in the house. Father's prayer shawl and many books, documents, my olive wood plaque from the Holy Land, even photographs, burned in the stove, filling the kitchen with smoke. The olive wood had a distinctive scent as it burned.

We did not have a mezuzah on our doorframe. We didn't join a synagogue upon arrival in Belgrade and deliberately chose our dwelling in a non-Jewish neighborhood, in the Kraljice Maria Ulica number 40. No one in the large building where we rented the apartment knew about Mother's conversion to Judaism years before. She had kept her Viennese birth certificate as a memento. Due to that we hoped that at least she had an opportunity to obtain a legal identification certificate and a food ration card.

WHEN I LEFT my home to go into the unfamiliar, I carried some art supplies and books from our home library to my hiding place. It took a couple of trips to carry the encyclopedia volumes. For almost four years in hiding, those books became both my company and my identity in that isolated rural area. In a way, the books were a substitute for the other missing essentials I had abandoned. The lack of thinking and interaction was as depriving as my hunger for food.

MEMORIES ARE NEVER entirely gone. They reappear, often not triggered by anything significant, not always predictable, like a strange change of weather patterns catching us off-guard when we are not wearing the appropriate attire.

RECENTLY, I VISITED my children and grandchildren in Israel. It was summer and there was smoke drifting onto the road I traveled. Brush fire, a frequent summer hazard, must have reached one of the olive groves in the Carmel Mountains. The trees were not visible from the road, but the familiar scent of burning olive wood was unmistakable. A surge of memory.

Israel, that ancient land and its traditions to which I belonged, had evolved. After millennia, the reborn country was an emotionally exciting place, where I could build my new existence. A home upon ancient ruins, an idealized sentimental base with which I, like so many expelled or unwanted others, identified. It was an easier task for us young people to construct a new life. The older survivors of persecution seemed so disoriented. But even we, the young refugees with less emotional baggage, found ourselves at a loss when we were isolated and not really accepted by the local community. We were called the newcomers and therefore constantly reminded of our past while paradoxically we were told not to talk about our experiences. Maybe our stories were too painful to be heard, and so no one wanted to listen. We were repeatedly told to forget our past. Perhaps the locals were afraid to face veterans who had outlived mass murder, mayhem, hunger, cold, isolation. We survivors stood in stark contrast to those who were spared such experiences. We were people of frightening memories.

It was a bizarre comfort to live in a place with so many misplaced, expelled, physically and emotionally displaced newcomers. Though we were living in close proximity, we came from different lands and diverse backgrounds, with different languages, habits, and accents. We were trying to establish a common ground in order to belong; it was challenging. All of us knew how it felt to be labeled, unwanted to the degree of being discarded. We carried memories that became indelibly perpetuated in our disconnected creative energy. Most of us immediately plunged into this newly discontinuous reality. In spite of emotional scars, some of us could maintain our personal assertiveness. Some were treading waves through rough currents, fixed in the same place. Some drowned.

No one was talking about those who committed suicide. Maybe our reluctance to deal with someone's suicide is innate. We cling to life. During the war it was persistently in my mind that I could be discovered and killed. I wanted to live, to discover what life was about. I did not understand giving up the option to reach old age.

There were suicides among the wartime survivors of my generation. One was my former classmate from Novi Sad. We had the same given name, but we were very different. I was outgoing, at times an audacious teenager, while Eva Smetana was really quiet and well mannered. We were not close friends, but she was part of the group of Jewish girls in the class with camaraderie and trust in each other. We reconnected at the Jewish community center in Novi Sad after the war. I knew that her entire family had been killed, just like my father and grandmother in Auschwitz. Eva was seeking my company. Maybe she felt the need to talk about her loss, yet she never did. Eva had married her boyfriend Ruben Lederer whom I remembered from our grammar school

days. My friends were preparing for the first departure of the Jewish sur-
vivors from Yugoslavia emigrating in 1948, to British mandated Palestine,
when Eva asked me for help.

IN 1944, WHEN the Nazis' deportation of Hungarian Jews to the
extermination camps began, Eva's father revealed to her and her brother
where in their house, concealed under coats of plaster, was a cache containing
gold coins. Eva, the only survivor of her family, and Ruben her husband,
recovered her possession. She told me they both concluded that I was the
right person they could trust and ask to help them take their property out of
Yugoslavia. Eva remembered that I always had ideas about how to overcome
problems.

Since their marriage, Ruben's family lived in the house. Furthermore, an-
other of our former classmates, Lea Rakosh, and her sister Tessa, who was a
year or two older than us, shared Eva's house. When in Novi Sad, I was also
an invited guest. It was in this house where I met Tessa for the first time. Eva,
her husband Ruben, Lea, and I were in the same class in grammar school.
Tessa, stricken with polio, spent those years mostly in hospitals. She under-
went operations to stabilize her knees so she could eventually stand and, with
the help of crutches and a firm body corset bracing her spine, walk a couple
of steps within the home. Otherwise Tessa was bound to her wheelchair.

When in spring of 1945 in Novi Sad the German and Hungarian Nazis
were rounding up the remaining Jews for deportation, a soldier left the hand-
icapped Tessa on the top floor apartment where the Rakosh family lived. The
soldier threw Tessa's crutches and wheelchair down the stairs, leaving her
on the top floor. After a couple of days the venerable survivor Tessa crawled
down the stairs several floors to the street. She found her badly damaged but
essential wheelchair. With the help of strangers, Tessa survived.

NOW, WITH THE prospect of leaving Yugoslavia and traveling to a new life
in the Holy Land, Tessa seemed to me the only enthusiastic person in Eva's
house. During the Hungarian rule of the Novi Sad area, Tessa had studied
art. She was talented, very disciplined, and extremely determined to be an
art teacher.

Eva suggested that Tessa's battered wheelchair represented the best possible solution for taking her gold coins out of Yugoslavia. That was why she asked for my cooperation. The wheelchair was constructed out of hollow metal tubes to diminish the weight. I was asked to distribute the coins within the hollow tubes without obstructing the balance or proper functioning of the wheelchair. Furthermore, if the wheelchair were lifted or shaken, there should be no sound of metal on metal due to the shifting of the coins. Finally, Tessa had to be able to turn the wheels in the manner she was used to.

I succeeded in distributing the weight evenly, thus the wheelchair was leveled. There was not the slightest sound as I wrapped each coin in tissue paper and stuffed all the hollow pipes firmly with paper before securing the round end covers of the metal pipes. There were no visible signs around the closures, even under close scrutiny. The tattered condition of the wheelchair's many repainted layers helped to disguise my additional intervention.

The next part of the plan was for Lea and Tessa to not travel on the same transport as Eva, her husband Ruben, and his family. Eva was the one who grew up in a wealthy home. The Yugoslav authorities were especially thorough in searching the luggage of the formerly affluent Jewish emigrants. Inspectors were present when we were packing the crates we could ship, to arrive after a couple of months. When I was crating my approved books, the inspector took out one book from the complete twelve volumes of the *World History*, mutilating the Franklin-Révai edition printed in 1869 in Budapest. I didn't protest. My only power was in being mute. I had learned that when intimidation has no response, the perpetrator remains deprived of satisfaction.

BEFORE THE FIRST transport got on the way, Eva told me of her apprehension concerning Lea's reluctance to leave Yugoslavia. I had my suspicions about Lea. She didn't show any enthusiasm about starting a new chapter of her life in the place where we Jews could eventually be more than a tolerated minority. Maybe Lea did not want to take care of her well-functioning, yet disabled, sister. If there were other reasons they were unknown to me. I promised Eva, before she left in 1948, that I was going to bring Tessa and the wheelchair. Eva's suspicion about Lea staying in Yugoslavia was right. As our travel time approached, Lea simply refused to leave.

When I obtained the travel papers for the second transport, as I promised Eva, I physically carried Tessa and my mother carried her wheelchair through the entire journey, throughout the two-day train ride to Rijeka, transporting us to the freighter *Radnick* in the port on the Adriatic, and the five days' journey to the Haifa port on the Mediterranean. My mother had no idea what was hidden inside the wheelchair's frame she was carrying. When we arrived, Eva and Ruben took Tessa, her suitcase, and the wheelchair.

IT WAS THE summer of 1949; the State of Israel was already declared. Within Israel our lives moved in different circles. We were building our professional and private lives and there was not much contact between us. A couple of years later I heard about Eva's suicide. It left me very sad. I thought she already had her new family, her professional and social spheres. The news about Eva's death made me realize how painfully little I understood life.

I really didn't connect to the former Novi Sad group, who mostly settled in the suburbs of Tel Aviv. Maybe the past was already firmly stashed within my memory compartment. The present was developing extremely fast, demanding my full attention. I kept detached from any particular social group. By that time I had given up the need to be accepted. I no longer searched for recognition by trying to fit into an existing mold with the prescriptive codes of behavior and attitudes of the surroundings. I was not going to belong anywhere. The profusion of prewar memories and the experiences during my hiding created my pivot. I was clearly expressing my state of mind. I was aware that at a time of building the future, there was no space to deal with our past.

That my husband Isaac completely understood me was enough. He accepted my past powerlessness, which left me reluctant to connect to others. At the same time, I maintained my drive to find beauty in the world around me. Through that perseverance, even in the despair of my teenage years, I was able to find beauty. It was in hiding that I had started to form the ground I was able to stand on, and hold on to life.

Surviving the Holocaust that had spared so few grew to become my backbone, influencing my lifelong thoughts and deeds. I had believed it was my nature that produced spontaneous decisions, whereas I realized later that my actions were led by profound obligations I was taught early on and would not abandon. Because I was enjoying living, which cruelly had been denied to millions of others, the difficulties of coping with my ongoing problems seemed trivial. By comparison, the war had dwarfed any postwar hardships.

Upon moving to Israel, I relished the bright sunshine, the sand, the sea, and the olive trees on the hills that surrounded the tents of our refugee encampment. That first impression rendered my lasting emotional well-being. Although I easily established links with the natural surroundings of my new home, I felt reluctant to bond emotionally with the soil. The reason might have been knowing the history and constant battle for ownership of small patches of land, which were frequently saturated with blood. I almost physically felt the cruelty that soil had absorbed throughout millennia. My battle fatigue may have created the pacifist within my bone marrow.

Trees had always been my source of engagement, and I was seeking their soothing presence. In childhood I loved the sound and smell trees exuded. In my daily routine to fetch drinking water during the war, the woods between the farm and the water source were my time-space of calm. I made a pen and ink drawing on my best sheet of paper of the large oak I passed in those woods. Looking at my drawing always filled me with tranquility in my frequent anguish.

For me as a painter the natural shapes of olive trees often looked admirable, with bark similar to crusty lacerated muscles devoid of bones, connected by invisible veins in which life fluid flows, producing energy. In Israel my new home, the olive tree became a source of beauty. The intriguing shapes of the individual trees, so different from one another, made them anthropomorphic for me. The cut wood cross-sections showed fantastic designs, which inspired me. The olive trees added symbolic meaning to my new reality in this place with its versatile people. On the surface we newcomers were very different from one another; the similarity was our traditional heritage stored within our core. We were sinking our uprooted lives into this soil of Israel after the mythical longing for a home had been our mantra for centuries. Just as those mystifying olive trees had withstood periodic destruction and continued existing, we, like those scrawny trees, survived without much individual ground. We were like trees maintaining our existence in an arid, rocky surrounding, under harsh conditions, exposed to the elements—to drought or flooding rains—even surviving frequent fire.

Most past experiences are stored in my visual recollections. Retrieved memory images render a similar sensation like thinking about some of my finished paintings. I know them intimately and don't have the need to review them. Yet if I do look, I sometimes discover previously missed details. Maybe my observational angle at the present has changed.

Additional life events, maturity, and discovered historic information of that horrific wartime were piling up within my personal memory archive, often forcing the past to protrude like a living root that was sprouting and growing shoots out of a tiny crack in a busy street pavement. At times memories seem to have a separate autonomous existence within my daily brain activities. They simply float to the surface and I can never ignore their connection to long-gone decades.

I remember the images I viewed when the German Army withdrew from Belgrade in 1944, and I was soon after working in the documentary film studio Zvezda. We received the newsreels kept by the former occupiers, including those films which were extremely compromising. The German Army left in a hurry and neglected to take or destroy the highly incriminating material, films from the concentration camps and the mass murder sites. I have seen what is now in the archives for historians. Those images flooded my entire brain. I never can remove those deposited atrocities from my memory. We in the documentary crew were exposed to those films. From that horrifying ordeal I learned what absolute hate produces. It impelled me, then and there, to amputate hatred from my own system.

MANY DECADES LATER, I experienced more images from that same time and those places, as an additional layer adding to my indelible strata. In the 1980s I was introduced to Phil Drell by Merle Gross who interviewed me for the Shoah Foundation's collection of Holocaust testimonies, and we became family friends. In the home of Phil and Winnie Drell, I was privileged to see the extensive collection of Phil's exceptional lifelong photographic archive.

As a Second World War U.S. Army photographer, Phil Drell had the first glimpses and proofs of the unimaginable. These images were filmed by the young American cameraman of a small film crew accompanying General Eisenhower when, in the spring of 1945, the first U.S. soldiers liberated the Dachau Concentration Camp. Phil Drell's unique documentation is now at the United States Holocaust Memorial Museum in Washington, D.C.

In his extensive film reels and photographs, Phil took one photograph that is virtually imprinted on the inside of my eyelids. The image is a long-distance shot showing mounds of bare human bodies. The trained eye of the stunned young photographer noticed a dark object on top of one of the piles of pale skeletal figures. Investigating what he observed, he created a close-up that he later printed into a still picture. It represents what neither he nor I can ever forget.

Thrown on top of naked bodies that look like parched wood branches from a desert in hell is the small body of what may be a ten-year-old girl. She is fully dressed in a coat, long socks, and shoes; she looks asleep but will never wake up. She must have died in one of the cattle car trains of no return, visible nearby—trains, which in the zealous intent to transport and kill the remnants of Jews from Hungary, were of the utmost priority to the Nazi command.

AFTER THE SECOND World War, the debate about inhuman human nature did not abate. How was it possible that Germany, in the center of Europe, claiming to be the arbiter of culture, which produced profound thinkers, philosophers, artistic achievements in literature, music, architecture, advances in technology, could at the same time cradle, produce, and inflate distorted conceptions through pseudoscience, culminating in the most unimaginable conduct?!

Do we as a species so easily discard what civilization painfully achieved through millennia? It must be a very thin, brittle veneer holding and controlling our behavior patterns, because the civilized demeanor fell off so fast and was instantly replaced by a delusional deluge of hate, making the unimaginable possible.

Hatred must have been so overwhelmingly omnipotent that it blotted out all reason and logic. Maybe there was a pandemic, an extreme contagious mutation in basic decency that turned wanderlust into murder-lust, infecting the brain.

Perhaps a major part of humanity had fallen into a prolonged hibernation of thinking and feeling and the incapability to imagine the other, a different person. Perhaps like a periodically cosmic cycle occurring on our planet, it was an ice age of frozen imagination. Because if we, just for a short time, imagine a single human, alive as we are, with all that life represents, if we imagine instigating a single face going up in flames, it must create an inner outrage of wrongdoing. Maybe such imagination could stop murder. Imagining of horror could stop warfare. Imagining someone else suffering might have prevented the world war. Perhaps when imagination is absent, a major part of humanity falls into a prolonged trancelike state, which eliminates the desire to emotionally identify with the other and enables mass insanity.

There really is no rational explanation for the Holocaust. There are so many explanations and theories, and yet I cannot understand how anyone can look on at a living person being starved to death and then turned into ashes. How is it possible to prompt an average ordinary person to murder an enormous number of people of all ages?

If we only imagine one person burned, one life turned into a grayish-white residue of organic substance turned into ash sinking into the soil! I believe the earth refused to absorb such a concentrated mass of ashes, burned human lives from the camps, gaping hollows in the soil of so many mass murder sites' killings!

The soil of our tortured Earth must have reacted. It is against nature's innate striving for existence that might have activated and reversed the direction of air streams. Winds that create our climate conditions could have taken the ashes from the crematoria and whirled the horror substance high onto the upper spheres of our planet's protective life shield. That ash is still circling within those fragile, thin coats guarding our Earth, those layers which enable life altogether, us, to exist as human. The ash joined that isolating membrane to safeguard against the devastating extreme power of hate, adding an additional filter, which guards us from even our sun's omnipotent force. Without protection against any unleashed central force, our entire Earth may turn into a wasteland of ashes.

I will paint one day how strands of the Holocaust ash swirl and float around our planet. Like enormous streams of gray strings, the human ash, a reminder of the unimaginable, is circulating in our atmosphere. It is in the air I breathe.

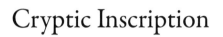

Cryptic Inscription

through our heritage we get a name

it wraps around us as a secure blanket

to snuggle in between expanding needs

we adopt the name as a frame of mind

form our identity

which alternately renders comfort sanctuary

or liability

depending on the rules of carefully predesigned snares

which at times will label us discriminate isolate

number us annihilate

if good fortune shields us from lethal scrutiny

we may survive disregarded

in anonymity

Battered and slightly broken, yet still functioning after two long world wars. Only an inanimate object can take such a beating and still erupt in energy.

I had always sensed that a story, which had existed in my mind since childhood, was connected to the weathered silver cigarette case that had belonged to my father. I remember how this case, in a brushed silver finish, had been an elegant receptacle for my father's tobacco. It was a necessary accessory in my father's daily routines.

Neither he nor his mother, our otherwise talkative grandmother, was willing to answer my questions about the inscription inside the cover or the identity of the person who gave Father that exquisite gift. Susan, my older and much savvier sister, didn't know either. No one at home ever told us lies, but there were subjects that were not discussed, at least not yet, we were told. At other times we would be firmly informed that our questions were inappropriate.

And so our knowledge of the family was stalled. Because my curiosity about an unfamiliar name on the inside of that case was ignored, I became even more inquisitive. I wanted to know who had given Father a gift with such a loving dedication. In Hungarian calligraphy, it reads:

Szeretett

Lacxi batyamnak

emlekul Doritol

1914 I 1

In free translation, it says, "With love, to my brother Latzy, in memory from Dori." The date underneath, January 1, 1914, is also etched in calligraphy. The entire inscription is on the inside and visible only if the case is empty.

In Hungarian, as in some other languages, the word "brother" is frequently used when talking to an intimate, a child, or a very close friend. Father was an only child. He had no siblings. Perhaps "Latzy" was a special name that this Dori, an abbreviation of Theodor, who in my mind became shrouded in mystery, had used for my father.

My grandparent's generation lived in an era and society profoundly influenced by Victorian habits about expressing emotions between men. Yet the word "love" shows Dori to be a man not at all reluctant to say what he feels. On the outside of the cigarette case is my father's engraved handwritten signature.

Even now, despite the passage of years, it clearly reads "Hegedus," the Hungarian name that father adopted when he chose to serve in World War One. The original family name was Herschel—not the right name to receive a commission as an officer. This was the explanation I was given when I wanted to know why Father's family name was different from that of our grandparents. This was a story whose details I was not too young to absorb.

I was told about the Jewish brigade of able Jewish men from Novi Sad and the surrounding region, which my father had joined as part of the Austro-Hungarian Army to fight for Kaiser Franz Joseph. All the talk that made history resound in my family's life could not, however, fill the silence about Father's silver tobacco case. All my attempts to clarify the inscription fell on deaf ears, building on silence. I spun the secret into a mystifying web. As I was an ardent reader, my imagination conjured an uncle who was connected with some clandestine, dangerous, and of course important endeavors.

The secret, I believed, was kept for Dori's safety, as I created him as a sort of emissary with a mission. I loved heroic stories; thus they featured in my fancies. The puzzling silence emanating from both Father and Grandmother became part of my history. I had at that time anticipated only praise for having learned to read before school age, especially in Hungarian, which I did not speak at all. My family's choice to ignore my question was baffling also because the explanations were often more elaborate than I wanted or needed, and I was obliged to take them at face value. In this particular instance, their unease and avoidance increased my curiosity and encouraged me to continue to probe. I not only had no success with Father and Grandmother, my mother was vague as well.

All I was left with was an elusive response to my questions, which from time to time rekindled my interest. Like some familiar tune replaying in my mind, but whose name evaded recognition, it became an irritating annoyance. The silver case was an unresolved riddle, involving my past two generations. I felt the cigarette case glaring at me from the pocket of Father's unbuttoned vest, his casual wear at home. Only in really hot weather would he take off his vest and wear his shirt with the extra starched collar unbuttoned and without the bow tie. I was proud of my dexterity, and so I learned to tie a bow. Even as a young child, I was very much aware of how Father dressed, especially in front of us girls in the house, including my sister Susan, five years my senior, who was to me a grown-up lady, and our live-in maid Paula. Father was always elegantly dressed whenever I saw him. The cigarette case was more than a symbol of Father's careful attire; it had become invested with my memories of him.

I ARRIVED IN my hometown of Novi Sad in 1944, after the German Army had retreated from occupied southeast Europe.

Paula was the one who gave me the sterling silver cigarette case. No one expected me. My appearance was a surprise. I was not supposed to be alive. Everyone I encountered upon my arrival in Novi Sad assumed that all the Jews of Serbia had been destroyed. No one knew that I had survived four years in hiding on a farm. The woman on the upper floor in our family house was a Mrs. Takatch, a frightened Hungarian widow. She expressed obvious relief when she realized I was not threatening her in any way. All I wanted was information about my father and grandmother, who during the war had inhabited the rooms on the lower floor. Despite her fear of me, Mrs. Takatch provided me with some details about how my father and grandmother were taken away. I had already seen how the beautiful parquet floors of the lower living space, where Father and Grandmother lived, had been demolished and replaced by stables. Before Mrs. Takatch spoke, I already knew I would never see Father and Grandmother again.

Mrs. Takatch also showed me what my father and grandmother gave her to hide before they were deported and killed. I made it clear to the woman that I had not come to take anything, not even that which was my legal property. I did not have the desire or the space in our shared apartment in Belgrade for furniture or other household items. I was only going to take what I could carry; war had taught me that lesson. This is after all what one owns after four years of war. The woman eagerly opened her cupboards, where she kept my father's and grandmother's clothing and other items for safekeeping. She also lifted her own large carpet to show me where our Persian rugs lay hidden underneath. Mrs. Takatch was as honest as anyone could be in the wartime chaos; that much was obvious.

Paula, on the other hand, was clearly suspicious and afraid of me, noncommittal and only slightly more relaxed after I gave her my father's clothing, which she indicated would fit her husband.

Though Paula remembered me as a spoiled child, she now faced a weathered veteran who reappeared out of another reality.

Both the widow Takatch on the upper floor of the house and Paula, who with her husband lived for decades in the cottage at the end of the garden, feared I would reclaim the entire property and want them to move out. I wished neither to return to the small town where I was born nor to settle within those now bare walls. Before the war this had been my home, but it belonged to a world that was irretrievable.

My goal was to study a creative profession and be independent, not to burden myself with futile responsibilities. Owning real estate was a costly luxury in the new totalitarian postwar state, and I realized that my only security lay in what I could create and from which I could make a living.

Paula gave me the photographs my grandmother left with her and my father's now indented and cracked silver cigarette case. I was grateful for everything anyone returned. I only took one of my father's suits for myself. It was off-white, a very thin tropical wool that no one could or would dare to wear at that time. I made it into a suit for myself four years later when I left Yugoslavia for Israel. I could carry two of our smallest Persian rugs. They were delicate and lightweight, so densely woven I could fold them like a parcel. All other things felt utterly meaningless to me. I was brought up to appreciate beautiful items and at the same time not to crave possession of them. This is why, even today, I can part with what I like and hold in my memory what I love. This freedom from ownership is my war profit.

As soon as I arrived in Israel in 1949 I sold the two small Persian rugs. It was easy to relinquish the beautiful weaving so that my mother could have a secure place until I found work. Years ago, I gave the United States Holocaust Memorial Museum some drawings and a small painting I created during the war years. There was no hesitation or any emotional ambiguity in parting with my intimate documentation of that traumatic time. I felt no need to hold on to images representing events that remained clearly in my mind.

Now I am about to part with my only existing memento of my father, his silver cigarette case. Again, it is not the object as such that provokes my hesitation. I keep that deeply tarnished case wrapped in soft cloth in a box, and only take it out infrequently. Safekeeping it for decades, giving it to a Holocaust museum, transforms that memento into a testimony of its own. Familiar objects often trigger a range of our memories. Unknown artifacts evoke curiosity, at times fascination, arousing our imagination. Father's cigarette case represents a profound personal feeling. The spring snaps open and the inscriptions are easy to read; they bring back an array of thoughts which sprouted in my childhood. My craving to understand the complexity of my surroundings was the first step in an urge to discover my own self. Of course that intricate task to decipher my personal enigma, even partially, took decades. My early life quest, to connect Dori, the unknown name, to my family relationship may have initiated my interest in the search to fit snippets of events into a whole, thus building up a construction that holds me together.

Out of those distant events, like the cigarette case, another closely related piece of puzzle emerged. It was our heavy brass Hanukkah menorah, one of the relics Grandmother cherished. Tradition in our family was perpetuated through her. The exceptionally large menorah was a family treasure that only Susan and I used to polish from time to time. Because Paula was not Jewish, Grandmother said it was not her responsibility to take care of our ritual objects. To enhance the candelabra's luster before the winter holiday of lights, Susan and I always gave the buffing more attention.

As the Nazi occupations expanded in the late thirties, some members of our rather distant family branch, the Weltman family, decided to emigrate to British mandated Palestine from Yugoslavia. We did not have a particularly close relationship with them, so it was surprising when Grandmother told us she was giving them our menorah. She felt the Holy Land was the proper place for it.

Susan and I were probably disappointed about the loss, so Grandmother clarified her motivation. She finally provided us with the story about the Hanukkah candelabra and explained her reason for parting with it.

In her youth, after one of the frequent pogroms in Eastern Europe when a Jewish village was destroyed, a very close friend had salvaged that menorah out of a burning synagogue. He carried it through many battlefields and upon his return brought it to my grandparents for safekeeping. We do not own the relics from our Jewish past; we habituate ourselves to treat them with reverence, Grandmother emphasized. That menorah must have been lit for Hanukkah throughout many generations. Grandmother's face had a surprising glow, telling the history of our menorah. We of course wanted to know who that brave man was who carried with veneration the symbol of our ancient history. It must have been a heavy burden during the war. The man's name was Dori, Grandmother said. Her voice made it clear that she had finished the subject. Susan and I turned to Mother, who said she remembered Dori as a close friend of the family who died some years ago.

Political events in Europe were piling up like a relentless snowfall with no reprieve. We saw it massing into an avalanche that covered the continent, burying humanity in a frozen inferno. Prior to the invasion of the Nazi Army, my parents and sister had moved to Belgrade in the hope that we would eventually have a chance to blend into the anonymity offered by a big city. I stayed with Grandmother in order to finish my junior high school class in a familiar environment.

There were already Jewish refugees from Poland, which had been overrun by the Germans from the west and the Russians who occupied the eastern part of the country. I heard about horrors taking place since the war began. My teenage years were already overloaded with the reality that was approaching and even I understood how powerless we were to avoid it. I was given the choice either to move immediately to the big city or to stay with Grandmother in Novi Sad until the end of the school year. I felt that to be with her was an exciting opportunity to have an intimate and undisturbed time with just the two of us in the big house. Despite her being such a very private person we had a close relationship.

My decision proved to yield a rare experience. It was like Earth's atmosphere, when there is a sudden calm before a large storm breaks, a clarity of color, a cessation of breeze when even birds seem silent. I carried this oasis of tranquility in my consciousness for life, that precious period of togetherness yet being separate. And to have that memory helped me through the long years of hiding during the war, as well as in the decades that followed. Before we parted, Grandmother told me that my father was her fifth child after four stillborn babies. I probably expressed sympathy for her losses, but she said that in her youth, infant mortality and stillbirths were frequent and it was always a matter of luck if mother and child survived. I was somewhat unaccustomed to Grandmother talking to me as if I were a grown-up woman discussing genetics and intimate relations: "There is vital importance to inform ourselves as women about innovations in the field of established knowledge, and most certainly get honest information. We know hereditary inclinations such as talents run within a family. But there are health hazards in marrying even a distant relative. Search for proven scientific information before making important decisions. We live in an exciting time of discoveries in some fields of nature, our nature." She knew I was reading what was in our bookcases, including literature dealing with natural selection and genetics. Grandmother insisted that I be aware of dangerous misinterpretations of biological facts derived from half science. She warned me about the Nazi propaganda that fueled their political lies. Grandmother was a well-read, informed, and sophisticated woman who could speak openly when she chose to. I was honored to have been considered an adult by her, to be able to talk openly. It must have been obvious to her that we might not have another chance to share such a precious time. She let me know how much she had enjoyed my stay with her, and particularly underlined how happy it made her to realize I was already mature enough not to ask questions that people will not answer. We both knew what she was referring to.

AS A SMALL child I started to draw people, and human expressions remained my creative theme through my life. My paintings are mostly faces and expressions of the body moving dynamically, uniting, distancing, or colliding with others, expressing the rhythms of random life. Some of my paintings are portraits of those who shared events in the many decades of my experiences. There are those calm and friendly features from peaceful seasons. Some in veiled tender loving emotions or others showing a blatant fear during the era of chaos and destruction. Themes recur like the refrain in an unending dissonance of the time. There are also many empty stares of confrontations with disappointments, as well as detached figures in a frequently lonely stalemate of midlife.

I also paint the perpetuating motion of my never-vanished ghosts, glowing with the effervescent energy they exude as they became the symbiotic flora within my brain, helping me to process that forcibly ingested venomous past that didn't kill me but left me with some immunity against the poison of hatred.

Some of my figures have their faces turned away so that I only see their shadowy contour and have to reconstruct through their movements what they might have meant within the vast canvas of my lifetime always rolling on. What I paint, say, or write is just part of what I can perceive and therefore express. It is a fragment, a small detail of a whole of that ongoing composition I cannot accomplish as I can never understand it. In the same way, I am only the sound of one musical instrument within a variation on a perpetuating theme.

IN CHILDHOOD I wished I had a face for the enigmatic Dori. Later I became aware of a shadowy inkling of his presence in my paintings and recognized him in many hidden forms. I feel honored to have had so many opportunities to polish the Hanukkah candelabra he had carried through the battlefields as a gift for my grandmother.

WHEN I AM excavating the dim shafts of my memories, I often sense a glimpse of life, distant in place and time, like looking at strange creatures in a far ocean depth, who exist in complete darkness. Because nature compensates in that lightless impenetrable unknown, it provides a different energy source to illuminate the swift ghostly sights of life from the abyss of the ocean. That is where our invisible beginnings began pulsating in the rhythm of existence. Memories feel to me visually similar. I experience my past like viewing instantaneous events flashing by, and I am fortunate if I capture some of them in my interpretations.

AS I HOLD my father's cigarette case, it evokes in my mind the long gone past; my childhood. Thoughts energize, making me eager to look through and beyond what was kept unanswered and therefore produced my undiscovered, obscured mystery.

Dori is part of who I am.

sounds surrounding

pounding rhythm of heartbeats

sights of life engulfing

smell of childhood shelter

touch of love

sounds of dominant encounters

followed by awareness and growth

sights of needs and urges

smell of budding splendor

touch of awakening

sounds of challenging choices

reaching decisions

sights of accomplishments

fragrance of mellowing

touch of time

sounds from dwindling ability

accepting secrets of the hidden self

sight of insights

scent from remote memory

touch of love

Antiquated Self-Portrait

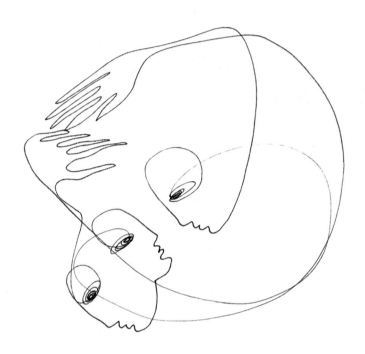

simplicity

an obsolete cell that can disintegrate

or expand into an intricate substance

exist divide grow a configuration

incite rational function

that might bear relation

forming a most complex entity

I am again about to move. Maybe this is why the backgrounds in all my self-portraits are so different. The backdrops in my life changed at a speed that did not match the rhythm of my identity. I am still recognizable in the auto-portraits through my many ages and stages and this is due to the bone structure of my cranium. The facade becomes worn, yet the structure remains. I still wear some of my olden clothing as each piece feels so comforting, intimate, saturated with memories. Aging, after a couple of years feeling satisfied with the stability of a routine, I spontaneously decided to travel.

As a painter I have a lifetime of work representing me. Everything from the periphery to the core reverberates through whatever I do or create. These results show who I am or at least how I view myself. In hindsight my slowly diminishing eyesight has softened the sharp-edged events, and by now the brush strokes of time allow me to indulge in memories. The numerous painful experiences are distanced, the joyful ones I keep accessible in my mind. I view my past like layers of cross-sectioned sediments and decide on which strata to concentrate. Retrospect becomes a comfort in my aging.

It still is what I do that delineates my priorities. I am a member of the Hidden Children of the Holocaust, a group of child survivors from around the world who, each year, travel to a different place to meet.

Most of us who survived the Nazi onslaught were in hiding during the Second World War. A few were temporarily hidden within the underground resistance. There were the exceptional children who survived some of the camps. A peculiar bond of understanding exists between us who lived through the war as children. We have an instantaneous emotional acceptance and understanding of each other with little need to explain. Although born in different countries, being different ages, accumulating memories, growing up within diverse social or religious backgrounds, we identify with one another because we were imprinted with a similar lifelong mark.

I perceive those of us who were children in the war as tiny isolated islands scattered randomly in a vast ocean archipelago. We were minute specks on a world map, conveniently overlooked when political cartographers drew the international boundaries of casualties, in the olden days. Representing the embarrassing, insignificant war residue, we were ignored.

Some years ago, flying over on a small aircraft from Suva, Fiji, to Tonga, I was engrossed in viewing the tiny coral islands in the archipelagoes in the vast ocean. Specks of trees and shrubs were growing in a saline solution of life under nature's most difficult conditions. I felt related to those islands and their vegetation.

IN THE FOLLOWING decades most of my friends from that group of survivors traveled to their places of birth. I never felt the need or wish to revisit Novi Sad, where I was born and grew up before the war. I did not feel any attachment to the place or to the people who gave me shelter on their small farm during the Nazi occupation of Serbia. As the German Army withdrew, I left my hiding place but lacked the maturity to recognize how important those rescuers were in my survival. I must have been emotionally blunted. This numbness, an inability to connect to people, lasted many years, as only complete detachment from emotions provided me with inner security. I missed acknowledging the significance of the farmers' decision to give me a place to hide in exchange for my work. I live with my omission, my embarrassment in not showing more gratitude to them. My shortcoming and insensitivity is a troubling memory. I thought that the immediate postwar urgency to gather the most essentials of living required all the energy I had left. It was a feeble excuse.

Finding my mother, and knowing that I could take care of her, gave order to the wasteland inside me. The location of my initial home in Novi Sad in the immediate postwar period was a vacant, lifeless, meaningless space, mocking the past.

BY NOW IT is utterly remote when I try to understand the patterns of my behavior. When the war reached my home in Belgrade in 1941, I briskly, resolutely left. Father suggested that hiding would be my best chance to survive the Nazi occupation. At fifteen I walked away from my home and family. I had no doubt in Father's intellect and judgment, yet through the following decades I tried to understand my swift action. Had I trusted Father's logical evaluation? He knew war, having served during the First World War in the Austro-Hungarian Hebrew unit of Novi Sad as part of the young Jewish Brigade readily defending the empire of Kaiser Franz Joseph. After that futile four-year slaughter, my parents' generation found themselves in a man-made country, the brand-new monarchy named Yugoslavia. It represented a somewhat undefined coalition of differing cultures and languages, people of different beliefs and traditions, thrust into an artificial unity. For the period of one generation it barely functioned, but even before the next world war started, Yugoslavia began to disintegrate.

MY PARENTS' GENERATION, the veterans of the First World War, had to run away from their birthplace with or without their children. The new generation of the former empire was again marching and killing. Explaining my teenage emotional state after an eventful lifetime is similar to the task of reconstructing an ancient mosaic with missing stones. My vain, not quite adult brain was at that time in a haze, caught between history and naive imaginings about war, derived from romantic literature.

I did not understand the looming terror on our doorstep. When the unimagined madness erupted all around me, in a numbed but strangely disconnected state, I left my family. Maybe nothing can prepare us when all our emotional capabilities have to abruptly adjust to a one-hundred-and-eighty-degree change of our existing reality. War does that.

Of course now I view my entire life in retrospect, analyzing events and my reactions to the happenings of my formative age, the diminished emotional intensity of leaving my familiar way of life, going alone into hiding. I remember it because it puzzled me. I felt strangely empty of any feeling. This unusual state reoccurred during extreme events during the war. I welcomed feeling numb, not sensing pain or fear; it was helpful.

I WAS BROUGHT up to think logically. The entire family was going to hide separately. Later of course I realized Father's precise evaluation of the danger if caught by the Nazis. Unfortunately many Jews and the general population had ignored the warning signs. Father was a well-educated man, but how could he have understood what the statesmen of most countries had misjudged? Did my father act in response to sensing the unavoidable doom if we were caught, or was his the spontaneous choice of a soldier with battle experiences?

Maybe it was my own intuition that kicked in, and therefore I ran from the lethal force. During my hiding I did not understand the significance of my lost school years; there were too many other more visceral losses. Without being aware, I also irretrievably lost normal emotional and sexual development as a woman.

When the Nazi invaders withdrew, four years had passed, yet I had not grown up. I was just a worn and weathered teenager, unaware of my losses and scars. The wartime had caused a physical amputation actively preserved in my brain. Because I was not familiar with such a phenomenon, I could not understand it. Only later I realized that all experiences remained within me, an emotional appendix.

STANDING IN FRONT of my easel, paintbrush in hand, wearing discarded shirts from my husband, I always felt as if in the center of viewing outer and inner life stages, where I could recall existing memories and paint them on a canvas or paper. I felt the significance of my task. I knew how to illuminate my fragmented images, make them enter the spotlight and show the clarity of a particular detail, while the less significant elements of the same event could remain further in the distance, like a backdrop curtain.

PHYSICAL AND EMOTIONAL isolation during my formative period in hiding created an inner self-effacing routine. This seclusion developed into a balancing exercise I have practiced through my entire life, especially when left alone during rapid and challenging changes. Years later I comprehended how my experiences had become part of my nature. My disregard of an ongoing trying time is easier if I accept it as a momentary passing calamity. When I compare unavoidable mishaps in the present to hardships during the war, or the four years of the immediate postwar totalitarian regime, all resemblances diminish.

THERE WERE POSITIVE moments within the postwar period. I won a scholarship from the Zvezda Film Studio, where I worked while studying set design at the Belgrade Academy. I received a stipend to specialize in building sets for films. My coworkers elected me for the prize. I received a scholarship to study in Czechoslovakia at the Barandov Film Studios in Prague. In my feverish attempts to make up for my lost years of education during the war, I learned to build architectural models from the architect Alexander Josic in Belgrade. He had hired me for my free-hand drawing skills, and I gained technical skills from him. The stipend I received in 1947 was an overture for my future.

Barandov Studios in Prague were not damaged during the war. Czechoslovakia was seized by Germany and the Nazis committed harsh atrocities against the population, but the infrastructure and architecture were preserved. As much as the citizens claimed to have suffered during the Nazi occupation, for me the city and surrounding areas of Prague looked untouched by devastation. However, being young, I only perceived what was on the surface.

I WAS NOW in my seventies, in Chicago, a city where life's random flow grounded me. The instant I heard that the annual conference of our Hidden Children organization was going to be held in Prague, an array of images from the sketchbook in my mind started to appear. These recollections felt unimpaired and fresh, in spite of belonging to a long-gone period. I still have some of my drawings from late fall and winter of 1947 to 1948 in Prague. They remained in good condition as I had the opportunity to buy good paper and paints and charcoals that were available. For the first time after years of deprivation, I had good-quality material on which to draw and sketch. I was so excited that I stopped smoking and sold my entire stock of cigarettes which I'd brought from Belgrade. Balkan tobacco was highly valued and so I had enough money for the costly art supplies.

Age twenty-one, it was the start of my journey back to well-being. After years of interrupted education I was simply a student, attending, learning, and discovering life had not lost its fun. Simple pleasures were now unbur-dened of mundane responsibilities. I didn't have any anxiety; Mother was receiving my monthly salary from the film studio in Belgrade.

In Prague I joined the production crew of Aleksandr Ptushko, the Rus-sian film director famous for *The Stone Flower*, who at that time was filming another epic production. When he heard I was a Jewish survivor he became generous in teaching me his innovative ways in building sets. He did not use painted backgrounds like those used in the theater, which were common in the early days of filmmaking, yet his preference was filming in the studio instead of traveling to outdoor locations.

Aleksandr Ptushko was innovative as an artist. He used circular platforms of different sizes: a smaller platform on top of a larger one. The inner circle moved more slowly and held smaller-sized, detailed objects, while the larger platform moved at a faster speed and held larger and more detailed parts of whatever the background represented. Viewing the projected film, it looked as if the camera was filming on location. The effect was marvelous and the production costs minimal. Small-size models of scenery were a valuable al-ternative in trick filming. I felt myself becoming accomplished, partaking in those contemporary art discoveries. The cinematography at that time was in its exciting experimental stages.

My favorite theater in Prague was that of Jiří Trnka and his marionette show "Shpalitchek." It was a puppet theater, featuring an improvised show about an unruly puppet youngster telling the children in the audience his personal problems and asking them for advice, thus creating a dialogue, en-gaging and interacting in a free exchange of ideas. I knew this was a subtle political satire enveloped in an educational performance. Not knowing the language beyond the basics, I missed a lot of the innuendos.

What brought me back as a frequent spectator to that puppet show was the laughter of the grown-ups who were satisfied beyond bringing their chil-dren to have fun with the rambunctious puppet on the stage. I had not heard uninhibited loud laughing for many years. It felt so good. It brought back my prewar memories, when political satires were the only response to oppressive powers.

I loved every minute of living and working in Prague, of roaming through streets whose buildings exuded history, as did the crumbling tombstones in the medieval Jewish cemetery. All were in dire need of care. Walking over ancient cobblestones in the old town with its narrow streets, I was practically inhaling my own distant past. Everything felt so inexplicably familiar although I saw it for the first time. My excursions led through twisting narrow dark alleys and shortcuts through inner courtyards within the ancient Jewish ghetto of Prague.

This atmosphere reminded me of the story of the Golem, because he was created there, in Prague. It was easy to imagine the mystical figure of the Golem, which transformed into the mythical, fashioned in the alchemy of troubling times for Jews. The story of the Golem involves a rabbi's attempt to create an indestructible protector for the Jewish community. "Golem" in Hebrew refers to the transformation of a caterpillar into a butterfly. It was easy for me to imagine the mythical Golem hiding in the shadows of the poorly lit, densely built crowded dwellings of old Prague, while the faint dripping autumn rain made the ancient cobblestones glisten like precious marble. I could sense the need, in desperate times, for a magical hero. The Golem felt appropriate in these surroundings, conjuring my personal memories related to my own desperate time.

AT THE BEGINNING of the Nazi occupation of Serbia in 1941, I had to burn some treasured books from our home library, as they were connected to Judaism. Walking through the ghetto in 1947, I remembered how I tore the pages and illustrations, burning books in our kitchen stove.

One of those books was *Der Golem* by Gustav Meyrink, with lithographs by Hugo Steiner-Prag, which I very much liked and often browsed. The illustrations let me imagine the story, because when I tried to read the book I didn't understand it. Our book was one of the first 150 numbered copies, published in Leipzig, Germany, during the First World War. When the Second World War reached my home, in April 1941, I had to destroy the book.

IN PRAGUE, IN 1947, the tilted rusty fences surrounding the courtyards looked the same as the illustrations in the book. I was walking through what in my mind might have been the place where the Golem had been created. This triggered my painful realization that I belonged to a shared persecuted past, which felt timeless, endless.

THREE DECADES LATER, in 1960s Israel, where I had lived for some twenty years, I woke early one morning. While my family was still asleep, I took our dog for a walk. On the low stone fence between the front garden and the street lay a book. In Israel, people used to leave unwanted books where anyone interested could take them. The familiar-looking book cover instantly immobilized me. Suddenly I remembered how that hard cover took a long time to disintegrate in the kitchen stove fire in Belgrade.

For a split second, I was back at the onset of the war. That familiar-looking book cover was facing me, from the ledge. The gray-greenish linen clearly showed the title, in Gothic letters, *Der Golem*. I opened the book to see who might have been the previous owner, but there was no indication. I was stunned to find that this book in my hands that morning was one of the numbered copies, just like the one we had in Belgrade.

This volume is number 141, printed in Leipzig in 1915. I have no idea who in Tel Aviv left that book at my doorstep. The anonymous donor must have brought that volume to the Holy Land before the beginning of the Second World War. I am forever grateful to that mystifying book owner. How did he or she know what I missed, and would appreciate to have!

TODAY, THE REAPPEARANCE of that rare book in my life is still an enigma. Once again the Golem rests on my bookshelf alongside the encyclopedia volumes from my prewar home, which survived doom beside me in hiding. They are now in my studio in Chicago.

MANY DECADES HAD passed since my first encounter with Prague. The mere thought of returning to that place so far off in time created an unanticipated thrill. Suddenly I wanted to be there once again. I was never interested in returning to Yugoslavia, or having any reunion with any place from my past. There was no one left there for me to visit. There was no one in Prague either, but I felt a magnetic draw and curiosity to experience that city once more. Maybe it was a yearning to renew the emotions I felt there. My memory of Prague was that rare time in my adult life when I was only a student and felt unburdened about coping with mundane problems, at least for a short time. Musing about Prague was similar to the faded attraction of an almost forgotten love affair—the intrigue and stimulation of the senses searching for details, which make some memories exciting and rejuvenating. In my youth, for a couple of months in Prague, I had dared to be on vacation from the war's reality, perhaps for the first time recognizing the pleasure of being young.

A LIFETIME LATER and a couple of days prior to my flight for the conference in Prague, I started planning the practical aspects of my trip. My decision was to continue from Prague to Tel Aviv to see my children and grandchildren. Of course I was considering what to pack, as I usually travel light, which asks for the elimination of what I decide to be without.

Chicago has been my new home over the last decades. Walking through my beautiful neighborhood downtown, along Northwestern University campus shortcuts and close to the Museum of Contemporary Art, brings me to the fashionable stores of Michigan Avenue. That was where I saw a vermilion red hat. It was impossible to miss, the way it was displayed when I entered the alluring designer shop. The provocative shade was unusual and drew me in for a closer look. That hat was crafted from narrow suede leather strips sewn in a circular pattern to form the hat and brim. It was art and craftsmanship combined. I saw my reflection in the mirror as I tried it on; it was flattering in its perfect fit, and to wear it became irresistible. The hat was outrageously expensive and of course I bought it.

Traveling to the meeting in Prague I felt as if one of my favorite composers had written a triumphal march to accompany my journey. I sensed an inexplicably joyous satisfaction about my extravagant hat. Here I was, one insignificant survivor of an annihilating war. After many decades I was arriving in Prague for a conference of those children who were not supposed to exist. We were supposed to be erased.

The conference as always was held in a large hotel and it was crowded with participating survivors who, like myself, were eagerly sharing our collective memories. Very much alive, with joy, I made my entrance up to the registration counter, wearing my high-fashion designer red hat.

a nimble squirrel hoarding morsels

through scattered autumn leaves

in the city park

quivering bulging cheeks dark eyes alert

swift limbs climb to the nest

safe behind bark

we often meet in the tiny green speck

flanked by concrete

I from the heights of my dwelling

of glass and steel

I too have the need to conceal

the sparkling bounty of now

the way I feel

and store it all at onset of winter

passing by I look at you bustling spry

heap pleasures of life little sister

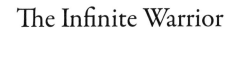

The Infinite Warrior

road dust tarnishes my overcoat

fading images bulge large pockets

crouching behind the sockets of my eyes

at dusk are swarms of memories

indulging me with versatility of my hectic journey

which is bound to cease sooner than later

and it does not matter

as my time span beside arduous difficulties

included an optimum spectrum of lavish hues

in genuine beauty

From a high point in the Judean Hills, the first view of the depression that represents the Dead Sea is an eerie, colorless, alien scenery. It is an abrupt transformation from a world of color into a vista of shades in not-quite-white and gray blending into black. It looked unreal and felt as if I were leaving the natural world, entering a monochrome lifeless formation of rocks with a faded, blanched brine on the far bottom.

I was looking at the pale moonscape that was not in a dark sky above me, but in a sunken crater deep and far away, and I was descending into it. The sun was on the decline, and darkening shadows, casting harsh, weird forms of sharp images on rocks, provoked imagination. On that winding road, the landscape, light, sounds, colors, scents, the entire air I was inhaling, had changed from the dry aromatic smell of pungent herbs on dry soil to hostile fumes of minerals. As we descended to that apparently lifeless area, the heat increased. A lone, almost motionless eagle was suspended in the air. Large dark ravens sitting like gargoyles on colorless rocks looked like painted brushstrokes.

Experiencing the Dead Sea area for the first time was for me the collision of history, prehistory, and geological occurrences retold in the scriptures. I wanted to discover which of those salt mounts looked like a sculpted female figure, the one who looked back at the past and turned into a pillar of salt. I was aware of the warning, of staying petrified in the time gone. I met some survivors of trauma who could not tear themselves from the past that had engulfed them like a spider's web. They remained immobilized, trapped, defeated, devoid of gumption to continue. I chose to hold on to the love that was given me in the past by so many who were taken from my life. As long as I remember them they are alive in my brain. I wanted to maintain all my memories, not to discard the depths of pain inflicted on me. Reality had taught me endurance and to a great extent how to cope with loss.

I WAS IN my late twenties. Accompanying me on this trip to the Dead Sea was my friend Nandor Glied, a Holocaust survivor, a sculptor who had been my colleague at the Art Academy in Belgrade. Nandor's sister came to Israel when I did, and it was she who told me about Nandor's plan to visit Israel. I understood why Nandor remained in Belgrade. During the Second World War, Nandor had fought with the partisans in northern Serbia. He was gravely injured by an exploding grenade. After many surgeries, several metal fragments impossible to extract remained in his skull. They were too close to the vital parts in his brain, therefore inoperable.

Nandor was the only person besides my mother in Belgrade I trusted. We were friends. Just before I left Belgrade, we had agreed it was better to be silent, as we knew that writing down our thoughts could have detrimental political consequences for Nandor. As a war veteran his health care was insured in Yugoslavia. I knew from his sister Manci, when we occasionally met, that his career as an artist in Yugoslavia was developing. He married one of our Serbian colleagues and had two children, his sister told me. All that made me happy. When I heard Nandor planned to visit Israel, I immediately said he could stay with us, as I had a spacious apartment in Tel Aviv.

My husband Isaac knew about Nandor's past, and of course was glad to have my friend as a house guest. Isaac, a promoter of arts in theaters, tried to introduce Nandor to established visual artists in the country, but at that time there was reluctance toward accepting newcomers into the rather exclusive group of those who made a living in the field of visual arts.

With all his artistry, Nandor could hardly support a family in Israel. Despite his entire painful past, embedded in his head, Nandor was enjoying being in Israel; he belonged. He would have loved to live and create in our challenging new-old country. Yet all of us realized that Nandor's prospering in Israel would be one more battle he might not be able to fight, due to his war injuries. We knew he would have to return to Yugoslavia.

NANDOR AND I arrived in Timna with the theater crew, traveling in the convoy of trucks loaded with the sets, costumes, and the essential stage lights needed for our work to prepare the stage. A historical moment. The Cameri Theater was going to have a performance of a local play on the shores of the Dead Sea.

The excitement we who were part of the project felt may have replaced the discomfort of the afternoon heat when we reached our destination. I was worried about Nandor's condition in the unusual blistering temperature. But he was in the same exhilarated mindset as we all were. I felt proud that my husband Isaac carried out his idea to have the theater perform in Timna, a desolate place, with only a few who could work under those conditions, on the lowest depression on Earth.

Arriving at the shore of this lifeless briny lake my first impression was of the silence. Gentle waves of a seemingly strange-looking, almost oily water were noiselessly splashing onto a shore forming a crystallized foamy whip that looked like an ill-prepared, unappetizing culinary attempt. Several rather corroded buildings and large machinery were half buried and caked with a grayish yellow mineral crust in the mud. Further down the road was a square newer building, apparently the offices and living quarters of the company's employees who at the present were extracting minerals from the Dead Sea basin. There, the activity of large equipment was in full swing. In front of the new building a small group of casually clad men stood around someone much younger in a white shirt and tie.

A tiny red curled ribbon was in the lapel of that man's blazer. He obviously was in charge here. The man had not taken the time to change his dusty trousers and shoes caked with pale mud. Timna was a rough place to work, but our effort to bring entertainment to these people was clearly appreciated. Working at the Dead Sea required competent, dedicated men with strength in will and limb; men with an ability to overcome a vast array of challenges.

In a short welcoming speech in Hebrew with a French accent, the person wearing the jacket and tie introduced himself as Jean Peer, the electro-engineer of the company. That was the first time I saw my next-door neighbor, who lived at 11 Lord Byron Street, Tel Aviv. My home was number 13. I was familiar with Bella Peer, this man's wife, and Danny their son. The boy was about my older son Ben's age and his playmate. Bella Peer, a grammar school teacher, taught nearby. Danny was almost daily at my home, because he liked the activities in my household. My entire apartment was mostly a working studio, with easel, paints, big rolls of canvas, paper and crayons, balsa wood and glue, driftwood, many books on shelves, and only the most basic furniture. I was building theater set models. I used to give the boys my discarded experimental models to paint. They were seriously working and I let them feel as if they were assisting me in my profession. They became involved and loved it. I could do my work. If they needed a rowdier activity the boys would play soccer on the unpaved street. There was no traffic, as the only car on Byron Street and its vicinity was owned by Danny's father, Jean, who was absent. Playing on the sandy street in the north of Tel Aviv was safe for children in those days.

Bella tried to explain the unusual absence of her husband, stating that his involvement in government projects kept him constantly away from home. When people seemed reluctant to talk, I never asked for explanations. The logical conclusion was that that Mr. Peer was in a line of work no government advertises. I met the enigmatic Jean Peer for the first time when we shook hands in Timna, as he introduced himself.

NANDOR AND I immediately recognized what kind of person we had met. Jean, this slender stranger who welcomed us, was of our generation. He must have been valiant beyond bravery in his recent past to have earned the hardly visible tiny cockade he wore in his lapel. The French Legion of Honor is the highest recognition for valor in France, Nandor and I knew that. At the present, this man was working in the most challenging of places in Israel. Timna was a renewed project to build an industry at the Dead Sea. Jean Peer introduced the men standing with him. We all shook hands before we were shown to our rooms in the main building. The sun was setting but it was still very hot outside. We were promised that the nights were going to be cool and beautiful. Indeed they were.

Because I was involved in the preparation for the next evening performance, I stayed up until the first light in the morning and sketched the wildly intimidating sharp edged formation of the mountains. Here, nature looked abstract.

This was to be the first theater performance at the Dead Sea since biblical times. After that short introduction, I didn't see Jean during the theater performance the next evening, or at the enthusiastic premiere party that followed. There were government dignitaries present, and many news representatives, as this was a national news event.

I started to think about the unusual encounter of Jean, Nandor, and myself. Close in age, we were linked through a war where each of us had been exposed to an entirely different survival experience. The common denominator was that, for each of us, our reality had been abruptly turned upside down. Further we shared our determination not to be caught and killed. We as Jews were outlawed, denied to live.

The three of us had defied and resisted the Nazi force. Jean and Nandor actively fought the obsessive fearful racist ideology, which had almost succeeded in annihilating the Jewish population of Europe. The four years of my war experiences were encapsulated in my memory vault. The three of us had the good fortune to have been in our teenage years, when the real challenges of adulthood are not yet fully developed, when life seems adventurous, fueled by imagination. At that age we could even, for short interludes, venture into the shelter of gratifying fantasy. We carried into our ordeals stabilizing prewar memories. Most important, we had good luck.

Now we met at the lowest depression on Earth, the remnant of a probably deep fiord, which in the geological past stretched inland from what at some time was a sea of reeds, now the Red Sea. When that water source tectonically disrupted, and the springs could not compete with drying heat through millennia, the death process of the area began.

Here we were, three young survivors of the Second World War, each in our cocooned personality, a decade after the Nazis' gargantuan mass murder. Out of a corroded past, Jean was building a viable industry at the Dead Sea, the most difficult of workplaces in Israel. Nandor, against all medical prognosis, was fighting a fatal disability by disregarding his discomforts and shortcomings, working in the physically demanding art of sculpting, creating and teaching a new generation at the Academy in Belgrade. I worked in Tel Aviv, in the theater, designing, building through sets and costumes an illusion on stage to enhance a literary reality. The impact of the Holocaust, an infection, was slowly draining from my system. I healed myself of the toxic residue through creating art. My paintings are a continuous expression and contain the tentacles of my experiences.

CARRYING THE BAGGAGE of memories from our recent past, in a muted din, the three of us were creating live projects from our awareness of massive destruction. Knowingly or intuitively we were resuscitating our inherited Jewish culture into an energy source for the future, our need to live unrestricted, to rebuild a viable, meaningful state of mind. Thoughts and emotions here at the Dead Sea bubbled to the surface, resulting in my uncommon, almost bizarre feeling that our meeting was not a coincidence.

It somehow had the aura of a symbolically staged occurrence. Maybe I was too profoundly immersed in theater. Yet the fact that Jean, Nandor, and I got together in the basin of the Dead Sea in Israel created a misty nebula I didn't understand.

I felt as if we were a closed, bonded society, silently linked. Despite the distinct backgrounds that each of us lugged around, we moved together as if in a designed pattern that we simply followed. On the surface it seemed logical; we compensated for so many murdered. I did not know what to think about it, but I surely felt the existence of a shared powerful strength.

Back in Yugoslavia I trusted Nandor most profoundly, whereas I did not discuss my political opinions with others. I was only somewhat familiar with Nandor's personal past; our friendship was based on the visual arts and our love for baroque music. We simply had an unspoken agreement not to let war memories interfere on the few occasions when we discussed our basic need of art, or the music after a rare concert. We would attend musical events, but we would stand in the highest galleries, as we could not afford better tickets. Now, a decade later, music had abundantly reentered my life.

One evening, after attending a concert in Tel Aviv, Nandor and I began to discuss the Nazi delusion of the thousand-year Reich. Our conversation took us to Wagner, the German composer who became a Nazi icon, whose music was not played in Israel. Within Wagner's series of operas, the Nordic god Wotan attempts to build Walhalla with the goal of reaching omnipotent power. The series ends with the inevitable "Dimming of the Gods." What a horrendous price, paid in human life, for a delusional maniacal paradox. My limited mind remained incapable of understanding how our supposedly advanced human brain conceived and carried out the annihilation of millions of our own species in the euphoric gluttony of mechanized mass murder in only eleven years. Those were the themes in Nandor's and my discussions.

WHEN I TRIED to imagine Jean's war experiences, I had only my memories of the newspapers during the Nazi occupation and the postwar film clips. The Nazis strutting on the Champs- Élysées, Hitler with a hideous grin dancing the jitterbug in front of the Arc de Triomphe, printed across entire front pages of papers.

I don't know where my neighbor Jean was during his teenage years or what his actions had accomplished. For sure they must have been exceptional, not only because he got the highest reward for his accomplishments, but because he did not talk about his deeds. This man struck me as someone fulfilled, self-confident, in control. In the heat of Timna, Jean's face did not perspire, his expression beamed with pride, greeting us when we arrived.

I realized the Dead Sea experience influenced my drawing. For the first time, I looked at nature and saw it as abstract. We look at death in an abstract way. The three of us, survivors of the Nazi dragnet, were very comfortable in this uninhabitable place, where the entire area exudes death, with few living creatures, dense salt water, and condensed minerals. Did this setting reflect how I viewed death? Was my familiarity with death due to an acknowledgment that part of me had died, and I had moved on? Had experiences changed me to such a degree that I transformed into a condensed compound of basics, like this body of water in front of me? Acceptance of death was part of the teachings from my childhood. Maybe Jean had a similar need, to be creative within a seemingly dead surrounding. Nandor was simply happy to be there. He was at home anywhere in Israel. Sadly he soon was going to leave.

AN ELECTRO-ENGINEER, Jean could have chosen anywhere to work. What motivated him to seek this location, with these extreme climate conditions, to express himself? It did not appear a logical choice, to hide, to be secluded. Perhaps it was what he was accustomed to, considering his clandestine existence during the Nazi occupation of France. Perhaps, even after the end of fighting, Jean needed a hidden, secretive, demanding trench. To me, Jean appeared as if one of the ancient emissaries, sent to secretly observe the land of Canaan. Jean emitted an aura of having discovered that milk and honey existed within his possibilities of accomplishment. We are all comforted by repetitiveness.

THERE IS A strange dynamic when war is over. The din of battle may be replaced by an eerie silence, while the brain does not regain calm. The brain, accustomed to the instant alertness, requires infusing the body with high adrenaline. When external stress subsides, vigilance remains, perhaps less intense than before. Some veterans turn inert, petrifying in an inner stagnant sea. Others have the need to share the still-ongoing past, as they cannot disengage from a bitter harvest of hurt. Our manifestations of behavior have as many forms and emotional hues as there are survivors of extreme experiences.

I ONLY UNDERSTOOD my own decisions decades after I had made them. When I encountered the puzzling Jean Peer in Timna, he radiated pride as if he had won a gold medal in the Olympics by working at the Dead Sea. Maybe that was how Jean wanted to live: with dedication, continuing under difficult circumstances, testing his personal endurance and discipline in an unobtrusive, most secretive way. Maybe he felt gratification when his assignments asked for utmost daring.

In order to absorb the Dead Sea experience, I was drawing on paper the unusual rocky crater. Time to review and hopefully understand my connection to the place, I hoped would come later. Maybe Jean had a similar need to be creative within a barely alive environment. It was a shame that Nandor was not going to live in Israel. His vacation time from the Academy in Belgrade was nearing its end. He and I didn't talk about another visit. When Nandor left we both knew it was for good.

WITHIN THE NEXT decades there were short periods when Jean Peer was in Tel Aviv. My mercurial next-door neighbor was mostly out of the country. Bella and Danny rarely talked about him and I did not ask. Jean seemed more visible whenever Israel was at war. During the frequent periods of existential tension, Jean Peer showed up in fatigues and dusty boots, like all the fighting men in Israel wore. In the interim tepid peace periods, Jean worked on projects abroad. When Jean occasionally happened to show up in Tel Aviv, Bella invited her circle of friends for a party. Jean did not seem to have any friends at those gatherings, but he always was the perfect host. Danny's frequent presence in my home increased when he became part of the musical activities my sons Ben and Raffi pursued. Danny with all his musical talent sadly did not keep up even with the discipline an amateur teenage band required in order to eventually develop and become professional.

Isaac and I liked and admired Jean without really knowing where and what this man was accomplishing. Jean was clearly a person giving his entire self uncompromisingly to whatever he was doing. Maybe his physical absence from the mundane routine of life, with its repetitive simplicities and fatigu-ing chores in maintaining personal family relations, was missing in the Peer family. Jean represented the most successful self-sufficient breed of loner I had met among those I knew who had survived the war as children. The post-death generation, forged in the randomness of an unforgiving time, we grew into adulthood on our own. Most of us developed abilities to give up but not give in to personal indulgence. Part of our personalities maintained the discipline throughout our lifetimes. My own inner need to exhibit order became clear to me as utter chaos took over.

THE ORDEALS OF the Second World War are distinct in my recollection. Maybe it was my upbringing, personal thinking, and decision-making that became the energy source from which I acted, rather than allowing inertia to incapacitate me. I remember I felt better as long I was active, when the bleak April 6, 1941, Sunday morning blue Belgrade sky unleashed havoc. Age fifteen, I did not understand that I was living in an era of dehumanization and mass murder. Perhaps some of the elders around me were aware of that.

I remember some of the tenants in our building from that time. Especially the family living on the prestigious large first floor, a retired general from the Yugoslav Army and his wife, both older than my parents, their son an officer, and their daughter married to a military man with their two-year-old son—Jokica, as everyone called him. I can recall the image as I looked into our air-raid cellar from the door. The expression of the grandfather, the aged military man's face, was of someone who seemed to be somewhere far away from the present. It was frightening to see eyes that viewed hopeless empti-ness. The two women dressed in black looked like motionless stone statues. Nobody was paying attention to the boy, who was hungry, I guessed, since he was sucking both his thumbs. I asked if they wanted me to bring some food for the child. The grandmother answered me. The door to their apartment was open and I would find food for the child in the kitchen, she said. Of course I went and cooked some cornmeal for the boy.

It took me years to understand that grandfather's gaze into utter void. The women shared similar expressions, both with a vacant stare, not allowing themselves to show emotion. Were they protecting the child, or petrified of loss? Later in life, I witnessed Israeli parents whose faces appeared to be cut out of stone as they buried their children killed by war. As I continued to paint, my work became imbued with pain and loss and expressionless looks, especially when drawing in black and white. I often feel as if I am a lightning rod, attracting powerful strikes.

I RESPECTED JEAN deeply. His prodigious past, fighting the Nazi war machine, earned him the prestigious award. His activities in the present were only known to us through Bella's words. Our generation did not flaunt achievements. On the contrary, it was viewed as poor behavior to brag.

Bella seemed content with her circle of friends and Jean's frequent absence. Jean was working in Iran, during the reign of the Shah of Persia, building large industrial government projects. Later on, Jean spent several years in West Africa. Jean moved constantly, apparently involved in complex building assignments. I saw no signs in my neighborly interactions with Bella but, apparently, through the decades, the Peer family relations were disintegrating.

After one of his lengthy absences, Bella told me that she and Jean had decided to divorce. To me, she seemed unruffled by this conclusion. Separations were not unusual among families in the social circles in which I moved.

MY OWN FAMILY life fundamentally changed when Isaac, my husband, suddenly died in 1978. Life had trained me in how to start anew whenever tranquility disappeared. I was in an emotional no-man's-land. All of my imaginative resources had evaporated. Isaac's unforeseen cardiac arrest was, for me, the end of emotional indulgence. I found myself in an unfamiliar inner wasteland. Work, my energy source, my best old tool, proved helpful throughout the mundane and in the face of losing the man I loved. At fifty, the passage of time was not in my favor, at the onset of my battle fatigue.

Nevertheless, I knew how to think on my feet. At the beginning of the 1980s I dared to expand my clientele beyond the few collectors in Israel. I even succeeded in having my work appreciated and purchased by tourists from Switzerland, Sweden, and the United States.

Opportunities in the United States slowly started to take shape. Tourists were accustomed to purchasing art that depicted the beauty of sunny landscapes, radiant watercolors, Galilee lake views, the atmosphere of the exotic, and the unfathomable draw connected to biblical roots. My paintings, however, were jarring, neither pleasing nor cheerful. They were memory items I was leaving as archives for future researchers. My artworks grew out of an emotional archeology—our recent painful history.

BACK IN BELGRADE, seemingly eons ago, my good old friend Nandor used to tell me that I was too naive (being a friend, he didn't say stupid) to recognize when I was defeated. When Nandor visited Israel in the 1950s, he brought me an enameled plaque with his drawing of Don Quixote slaying his own image. I still have this piece, Nandor's portrait of me, and the precious memory of him.

IN MY MID-FIFTIES, preparing for my trip to the United States, I traveled through Europe and visited the collectors of my work in Switzerland. Bella Peer, my neighbor, aware of my rather elaborate project, urged me to call her former husband Jean, who had settled in Switzerland. When Bella told him about my journey, Jean said he would love to meet me, as I was one of the few friends he enjoyed talking to. Bella gave me his phone number in Geneva, where he lived. I had never been to Geneva; it was an opportunity.

Usually I stayed in St. Galen, where my clients lived, and in Ebnat-Kappel, a short train ride away. When I called Jean, he sounded delighted, therefore I stopped in Geneva on my way to the United States. He had changed his name from Peer to Piernikaph, which I assumed was his family name before the war.

These were the 1980s. Three decades had passed since our first meeting on the shores of the Dead Sea. A lifetime ago.

Jean met me in the restaurant he had suggested for a late lunch, overlooking the gorgeous Lake Geneva. Jean had put on a little weight, I only extra years, with the by-product of sagging skin and aches in my joints. Apologetically, Jean said that the reason he did not invite me to his home was that his new wife recently had a baby. It was more comfortable for the two of us on the veranda of the restaurant overlooking the beauty of the lake; most important, this place served superb food. Jean was evidently pleased to see me. I had never seen him so genuinely relaxed. Jean didn't show me any photographs of the baby or of his wife. Of course I did not ask, just congratulated him and said it was wonderful that he had started a new life. Understandably, it was more convenient for all of us not to burden a new mother with the task of entertaining. Jean did not continue talking about his present life and I dropped the subject.

I knew that Jean had always avoided talking about his personal life, and it felt good to see him at ease. He deserved happiness, I thought, after all his former family disappointments, at which I'd seen him stoically smiling. He asked me about my son Ben. It did not surprise me because Jean always liked Ben and probably hoped that Ben's friendship would have a positive influence on Danny. I believed that Danny was a great disappointment for both his parents. I carefully curbed my own need to talk about my children.

JEAN AND I spent an absolutely delightful afternoon going over our shared political experiences in Israel, the theater, art. We belonged to that fortunate Second World War survivor generation, privileged to participate in building a new home in Israel, the new country against all odds. Surrounded by hatred, propelled by resilience developed through millennia of persecutions leading to a zest for innovation, Jean and I knew how to talk a lot about life, yet we omitted what neither of us wanted to mention.

Jean seemed not at all in a hurry to go home, which made me wonder. No one called him during the several hours we were sitting on the terrace. We tasted delicacies that Jean knew to order, knowing my vegetarian preference. We watched the swans gliding on the lake as we sipped wines appropriately paired with the foods served. Jean had always been the impeccable host, and I believed him when he said he appreciated our reunion. We both were too experienced and aged to simply smile politely as one does at parties. We had both had enough of artificial pleasantries.

On the shores of Lake Geneva, both in our new present, having this leisurely gourmet lunch, sipping superb wines on the veranda of a lavish restaurant, I appreciated the wonderfully slow-paced afternoon, enjoying the sparkle of the water, the swans, the unexpected randomness of our constantly dynamic lives.

THERE ARE THE rare fulfilling moments we at times enjoy without any preliminary or continuous repetitions. These can happen at a concert, in an exhibit, reading a beautiful sentence, experiencing an interesting encounter. Jean and I knew our entire life was an erratic turmoil of the unpredictable present existence.

THAT WAS WHAT Jean and I had always been, the children who emerged from the tentacles of the past. We had the good fortune to learn early on how to function within the turmoil by constantly adjusting to the erratic changes of life, while simultaneously maintaining our core. Jean was always involved in covert projects. I was once again starting my perpetual overt mission, looking for new locations to expose and exhibit what I felt was my firm obligation to say.

within the random draw in existence

our life is a faint glow

in the perpetuating strife

between erratic speed and obscured need

Ceasing Season

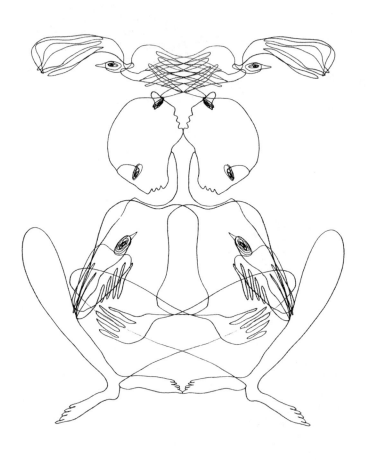

love

an ultimate short word

no heap of letters in any language does explain

how the brain leaps

determining intrinsic properties of our intricate emotion

at first glance lucent

as opaque evolvements are covert

in dim crevasses of our geology

growing hidden in coves

where energy fluid throbs

and drowns in overthrow the entire entity

or parched by drought starts to decline

into a shrunken shoreline

It was a new city, a new country. Even the language was too unfamiliar for me to start conversations and build sentences that would make sense. How does one express a fluent meaningful thought in a language one does not speak fluently?

Some of my ancestors were Jews escaping frequent persecutions, wandering from one temporary place to another across millennia. Maybe I am a descendant of the nomadic tribes from the far eastern steppes who through centuries periodically rode westbound, overrunning Europe. Perhaps there were romantic encounters of my foremothers with some of the minstrels throughout the past—those troubadours who were only allowed to camp outside the walled cities, furtively entering, hiding in the back alleys. When cities grew beyond the fortified outer walls, inner walls sprung up. Established were the restricted quarters for the "others," those labeled lesser dwellers, classified and isolated between the fringes of society.

And there were those who were not even allowed to settle in a ghetto within a city. The Gypsies. The horse traders, acrobats, artists, musicians, entertainers, juggling life, always on the move with the perfect pitch for survival. Those entertainers were hired to create a joyful atmosphere, amusing the few who could afford to celebrate. The performer's art was appreciated but the strange skillful wanderers were only briefly tolerated, offstage.

Over decades I frequently coped with being feared because I was a stranger and dared to bare my soul in my work and through my behavior. I feel in me that simple, maybe naive, unbridled need for freedom and I express sorrow or joy in my art. The nomadic trace in my DNA is evident.

I AM AN offspring from the fertile region, the river Danube plains, where all the known and clandestine invaders throughout history temporarily established themselves, leaving imprints. I carry in me resettlements, furtive escapes, forceful bans, and all those eventful adventures created by political greed. Generations slowly endure, weaving the tapestry of our history. Such an absurd reality might be humorous and entertaining if it were not saturated in blood.

Because frequent relocation eliminates attachment to firm ground, I probably developed air roots, carrying them within, where most nutrients exist in my ecosystem of nurturing memories. Decades ago, when my age was considered old for any new start in life, I was not deterred to venture on a new journey. With graying hair, sagging facial muscles, a widowed grandmother, I was answering an opportunity to start a new chapter in life.

My sons were adults creating their families. My daughter was in her late teens, and I needed to increase my income to enable her, after her army service, to continue studies at the university; I restarted a new journey against many odds. The challenges of a fresh project always enhanced my well-being. Several years after the death of my partner in love and life, my comfort at home started to feel stifling. It obviously was the end of a substantial period of my life and I had to create some innovation within my routine. The chance to exhibit my paintings in the United States prompted me to decide to see the world that I had only known through literature and the arts.

As a creative person I was continuing to overcome the overall assumptions that it was difficult for a woman to maintain financial self-sufficiency in the visual arts. I was not encouraged to travel abroad with my work. After all I was an unknown painter in the United States. I had no backing of well-established gallery owners in the capital art centers, or even a well-printed catalogue to send, and definitely no youthful vigor.

I HAD SOME clients in Europe who had bought my work when they visited Israel. I had a proposition from Beatrice de Ferrer Cohen, who started an art gallery in Darien, Connecticut. When we first met in the 1960s in Tel Aviv, Betty and I had developed a friendship and mutual admiration, she for my paintings, I for her highly musical abilities. Almost twenty years later, she wanted to exhibit and launch my work in her gallery.

Another friend from my early childhood, Ava Brownley, lived in Chicago. She worked in the travel industry and was eager to promote my art in her spare time. Our friendship dated from preschool. It had dissipated for years, but in 1945, at the end of the war, we reconnected. Ava Brownley was married and for years lived in Chicago. In the 1980s I had been a house guest at the Brownleys' when visiting in the city. There was a prominent gallery on East Delaware Street, which displayed my work on consignment.

Some art collectors had acquired my paintings. I was in the city when my work was shown at the Spertus Museum as part of an exhibition, curated by Grace Grossman, of Israeli artists owned by Chicago art collectors.

My oil painting arrived late for the show. The entire wall space was already filled. The Spertus Museum had the first public display showing the surviving Holocaust artifacts collected by the Spertus family. Ms. Grossman mounted my painting on the central column in the exhibition hall.

Ava Brownley told me in our phone conversation that, this time in Chicago, I was to meet someone who had bought two of my paintings and wanted to meet me. She insisted that I fly in from New York to meet the new collector of my work, during the oncoming High Holidays. She was not an observant Jew, but social events in the Jewish community were important for her. My agent in Connecticut, Beatrice Cohen, was busy with another painter's show and so I flew over.

I remember that late afternoon, looking forward to the encounter and to dinner. The hostess was a nice lady whose culinary fame was based on being the southern belle of gracious dinner parties. She told me she was intrigued by the challenge of creating a mostly vegetarian meal in my honor, which I thought was extremely kind. In the mid eighties in the States I mostly received a baked potato and soggy vegetables. She sounded excited to try out a new cooking trend and I was the only vegetarian she knew.

Here I was in Chicago, standing on the southwest corner of Wabash Avenue, looking at life moving over the many drawbridges, crossing the slow rolling river. In the east I could see the water of Lake Michigan covering the horizon like a sea. Water was my favorite element. This city had attracted me at first sight. Now I appreciated being surrounded by the fall sunset because it was a slow colorful ending to a day. The slanted, almost crimson light fell on the clean white Wrigley Building and partially the Chicago Tribune's Gothic spires. Straight across the river were identical twin towers. A circular, apparently functional design, as the buildings being at river's edge provided docks for boats and garage spaces on several of the lower levels. For me the intriguing design detail was the garage's steel cables as safety barriers, instead of walls. I tried to imagine how it felt to drive on the edge of a building where only thin steel cables protected one from plunging into the river. This was a boldly beautiful city with design innovations and diversity in material and form making distinctly novel statements in urban architecture. The present weather was exceptional in a city famous for erratic fluctuations. I liked that unexpected mutability of nature.

My friend Ava Brownley was busy with purchases at the corner drugstore. I deeply disliked browsing through merchandise, thus I did not join her. As usual she was going to be late for our meeting, but that was her habit. I had noticed the good-looking man standing beside his car, apparently waiting for someone as he looked at the entrance of the large office building where Ava Brownley worked. Fleetingly the man looked at me standing, observing. If this was the man who had bought my paintings, my friend failed to mention that he was very handsome.

He was slender and tall, wearing a well-fitting three-piece suit, had graying hair, and I imagined it would be nice if he were our escort for the dinner party. My friend did not say a lot about the man who showed interest in my work. I only knew that Mr. Schieber was a gentleman she had met at a meeting of Al-Anon, the therapy group for spouses and family members of alcoholics she had recently joined. Ava Brownley loved other people's stories. She generously used to tell me details of other people's lives. Because she worked at a travel agency, I heard stories about her clients I would never meet.

My friend's husband had suffered from alcohol addiction for a long time. So apparently did Nathan Schieber's wife. Ava my childhood friend and I shared the same given name but we were quite different. By now Ava Brownley was in her third marriage, and in the strangest relationship I'd ever encountered. If she had been having a secret affair with the man who bought my paintings, I would have understood, condoned, and approved.

What I found intriguing about Mr. Schieber was that he promptly bought two paintings the first time he saw my work. My amusement grew as the man who triggered my thoughts stopped looking at the building portal, approached me, and said, "Excuse me, are you Mrs. Kadishson?" He had a pleasantly deep voice, and I liked his relaxed attitude, interesting powerful face, and military mustache. As I affirmed, he introduced himself. He indeed was Nathan Schieber. We both had guessed right. I asked him how he knew who I was. Had he seen my photograph?

No, he said, but he had imagined the painter to be a woman who visually admitted to a powerful loneliness and therefore the artwork had to have been created by a self-confident artist, a person who does not care how others perceive her behavior. His broad smile was disarming. "You are standing alone, at ease, in the middle of a busy street, undeterred, with concentration, looking at the city's architecture. Now I know what I admired in your work. I wanted to see the artwork across my desk in the office where I spend most of the day." The man knew how to praise without flattering clichés.

He was observant, analytical, well educated, and eloquent. I liked that man. He recognized who I was by reading my paintings. After several years disregarding the opposite sex, I suddenly felt intrigued by a strange man. Nathan sounded pleasant, relaxed, and I was comfortable with his unconventional approach, not waiting to be formally introduced. There was nothing pretentious or conceited in his behavior. Nathan Schieber did not try to impress me.

My friend Ava was unintentionally late. I was rarely annoyed with her as I knew where her behavior originated. The damage she lived with after the Second World War had had a head start in her troubled childhood and this made me ever more lenient about her lack of logical behavior. On this particular occasion I even appreciated her tardiness. She obviously did not plan for Nathan to meet me like this, introducing himself. She liked to be in charge, which resulted in meticulous contriving, enjoying her influence over how people made decisions. In her work this was probably helpful in order to persuade indecisive clients to choose particular vacations or accommodations. Her need to control, however, by now turned into game-playing, marring her own life. Striving for an imagined elegance and etiquette always left her unfulfilled. I may have been forgiving of her due to my awareness of her self-deceptions since childhood. I had always given her a large commission from sales of my work. She had her name on my bank account in Chicago and could take a loan when she needed money. Quite often, she gave away my drawings as a gift for someone important, claiming that this would promote me as an artist. I accepted her taking advantage of that. Life had taught me there was a price for everything.

WHEN WE ARRIVED at the Rosh Hashanah dinner party, there were the usual drinks beforehand with appetizers, people mingling, and polite exchanges of pleasant words that we rarely remembered afterwards. What had registered in my mind was that Nathan was beside me all that time. It was as though he was shielding me. I felt amused, because I didn't think I needed to be protected.

I was in my late fifties. I had just met a man I wanted to be intimate with. It was somehow unexpected, sudden, and powerful to recognize my natural urges. It reminded me of my youth, and I was acting on my innate guidance as I did through my entire life.

That evening remains etched in my memory. I was in a tangle of familiar emotions, while my rational thinking clearly indicated that my age was not suitable for a romance, at the same time asking why not? I felt rejuvenated in the realization that I was still sexually a woman with natural reacting needs I thought were gone. I felt like a musical instrument, resonant and definitely not out of tune. I still was curious to pursue what life was apparently offering. And there was the amused realist in me noticing how the physical sensation of Nathan sitting beside me, his knee ever so slightly touching mine, evoked my sensual reaction. He eagerly kept our conversation flowing while not taking his eyes off me, and handing me things that were on the table even though I didn't ask for them, just to touch my hand. Was his behavior obvious to everybody around, or did it only exist in my wistful wishing to experience an Indian summer in late fall? Was this mature man, an American veteran of the Second World War, acting like an eager schoolboy? I thought so and loved it. But was I assessing reality?

There was the slight embrace in the lingering of his hands on my shoulders as he helped me into my coat. My entire body responded to his gentle hold and I wanted that sensation to last, as it was a pulsating invigoration. We sat in silence in the car on the way home.

WHEN WAS NATHAN going to call me after that evening? Was he aware of how I felt? He knew I would be in town for more than a week before returning to Connecticut in preparation for my next exhibit in Canada. Ava Brownley's kitchen table functioned as my Chicago studio, prepared for that oncoming showing.

Nathan called the next morning from his office. He was eager to see me. There was a lot for us to talk about, he said. His voice confirmed that I was not daydreaming. Between his words was his keen intention to continue our phone conversation. Voice had always been an indicator for me when listening to people. I would read the intonation and often recognize what the person who spoke left unsaid. I never understood how this was clear to me, but usually it was accurate.

Nathan felt for me as I felt for him, this was evident. We were drawn to each other the way teenagers become infatuated, experiencing a feeling that seems as if it had never happened to anyone ever before. Sitting in my friend's kitchen I was trying to concentrate on my reality. In a new environment, beginning a new project difficult even for young artists, now suddenly I was in love like an immature teenager. Of course I had to laugh at my surge of yearning to be with a man I had just met and did not know much about. I simply wanted to have him beside me, and the feeling was wonderful.

Nathan was calling daily. We talked about politics, books, the comfortable, impersonal. He was going to pick me up on Friday at five for dinner, just the two of us, he said. Until that weekend my days were in a haze. Amused at my youthful giddiness gone so many decades ago, I was realizing my own sexuality.

Nathan arrived, parking the car just as I locked the front door of my friend's three-flat. He moved hurriedly to open the car door for me. Beatrice my agent had in vain tried to teach me to act more feminine. She was desperate to make an American socialite out of me. As a lady I should always wait and let a gentleman open doors, she had told me. It was ridiculous to stand and wait not doing what I was capable to do. I laughed, Nathan looked puzzled, and I had to explain.

Nathan's answer reassured me, that he had thought about my attitudes during that week. He said my independence was exactly why he hoped to be beside me and open doors for me in the future. This man was funny and clear about what he said.

He took me to a neighborhood I was not familiar with. Andersonville was one of Chicago's distinctive enclaves with small boutiques, sidewalk coffee shops with Swedish names, and mostly young, casually dressed people walking their dogs. The atmosphere in this multiethnic city was different from the formal air in the Loop for Friday dining. Nathan assured me the vegetarian restaurant had been established years ago and was always crowded. The patrons around us were mostly young professionals as well as those by now not so young—the "flower children" generation, but even they were the age of my children. The rustic decor of the restaurant and the old trees in the garden with the fresh air were the starter to a delicious dinner. I felt comfortable in the absence of meat odors and fumes of burning fat and thanked Nathan for choosing this location.

When I asked Nathan about his war experiences, he was grateful and not surprised at my interest. He had not talked about those years, as nobody but another veteran would share the burden of war memories.

AN AMERICAN SOLDIER, Nathan was stationed in the Far East, including India, Burma, and China. Before he went to war, he married his girlfriend in New York, where both were born and lived. Returning to California when the war was over, Nathan called his wife, who said she wanted a divorce. She was in another relationship. Nathan stayed on the West Coast and sent his consent. Immediately after the war, in California, he started to work for the United Jewish Appeal, a fundraising organization that provided means for purchasing arms for the Haganah in the struggle to create the State of Israel.

I was watching Nathan's face, as he did not show any emotions while telling an array of revealing memories. I did not interrupt his calm, clear voice when he continued with more vigor to go into details about why he was eagerly working for the UJA. "The organization was of importance after we discovered what had happened. There was a great need to save the survivors and displaced, homeless, expelled Jews, and children left in orphanages." He was telling me what I knew, but I wanted to listen to his eloquent narrative. Nathan became passionate as he explained the reasons for his work.

His fundraising assignments continued successfully until 1948. When the State of Israel was declared, Nathan was offered an administrative position in a big manufacturing company in the Midwest. He moved to Chicago. "I was successful in business, not in my private life," Nathan added, sounding matter-of-fact. "In Chicago I married a divorcée with an eight-year-old daughter. She came from an educated, uncaring Jewish family. I thought my creating a comfortable home would work. I was wrong." A short sentence explaining a lifetime. I looked at this attractive bright man calmly disclosing, without a trace of self-pity, what one rarely admits to oneself.

Now with adult children out of the house and a separation there was an agreement for divorce, he said. The main reason why he took me to a neighborhood far from the glitzy restaurants was that none of the patrons here could be connected to his wife. "Through the years we had several separations. This time we have almost finished the proceedings. I have to be careful and not be seen dining with a very attractive woman. My wife's lawyers would greatly complicate the process and I want it solved. Now more then ever before," he added quietly.

NATHAN WAS ON the mend and wanted to be needed. We met on that crossroad. Two aging wayfarers each with an enormous ballast, war veterans of different but lasting experiences. Together, we both knew, nothing else mattered.

It seemed unreal, but I didn't want to analyze and understand. I just wished to enjoy the feeling of the moment. We sat and talked long after our table was cleared. In the car we sat silently, waiting. Still stalling, like kids not daring the first move. I wondered why we had not kissed. Nathan turned to me and asked simply if I would stay with him over the weekend. I said yes and we kissed. As we did, it was that seemingly endless fluid sensation, clear and unmistakable, wanting each other without delay. That gratifying experience, with no words, either questions or answers. Neither of us needed an explanation, it would have been superfluous, probably impossible.

experience of a rare reoccurence in late autumn

before daybreak

a luminous wrapping cape from the universe

an enchanting cloak around our minute existence

you are my moat to keep harm away

I am safe at last

dense darkness closes in

the day is gone like a fast stampeding herd

rest your head under the folded wing

migrating bird

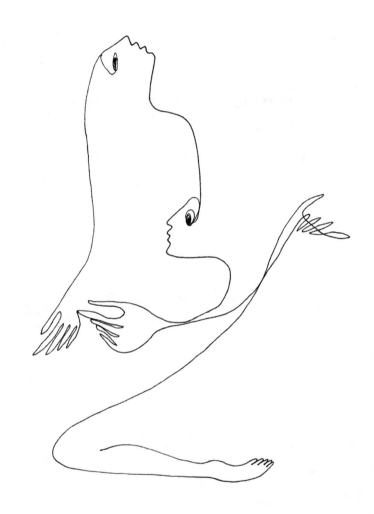

Ava Kadishson Schieber was born in Novi Sad, a city near Belgrade, Yugoslavia, and survived the Holocaust in hiding on an isolated farm. A Chicago resident for thirty years, she is the author of *Soundless Roar*. The focus of *Present Past* is her life after the Shoah. Rejecting stereotypes of Holocaust survivors as traumatized or broken, Schieber is stark yet exuberant, formidable yet nuanced. The woman who emerges in Schieber's *Present Past* is a multifaceted artist, a passionate observer who dispassionately curates the kaleidoscopic memories of her tumultuous personal and professional life in Belgrade, Prague, Tel Aviv, New York, and Chicago.